MW00365684

FERAL NATION
PERSEVERANCE

FERAL NATION
PERSEVERANCE

Feral Nation Series Book Five
Scott B. Williams

Lightning Struck Press

ISBN: 9781798962244

Cover & interior design: Scott B. Williams

Lightning Struck Press

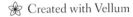 Created with Vellum

This one is for Flint.

ONE

THE SILENCE VICKY WOULD NEVER GET USED TO returned to the desolate ranch as soon as Eric was gone. The utter quiet out here was like nothing she'd ever experienced. It hung over the valley with an intensity that was palpable, and had been with her day and night, broken only by the wind whispering through the pines in the afternoon and the occasional yip of coyotes in the night. The stillness was always worse in the mornings, the silence virtually a vacuum that threatened to suck even her thoughts into nothingness. With no sounds of life nearby, either animal or human, Vicky had never felt so alone in her life. It didn't help at all that the shallow graves of her recently-deceased grandparents were just a stone's throw away from where she sat, alone there in the barn.

Situated as it was in such a remote part of the Colorado Rockies, the ranch was always a quiet place compared to the cities and towns where Vicky had spent most of her life. Too far from any highway to hear even distant sounds of traffic, the isolation of this place had seemed peaceful and inviting all those years before, during her summer breaks here visiting her grandma and grandpa. And after all that had happened in recent months, the ranch seemed even farther removed from the outside world than ever. Of course, that was why she and her friends came here to begin with; to escape the life that had fallen apart around them. Their hope was that it would be a safe refuge from the violence and confusion that had consumed every place where there were large numbers of people. Things hadn't worked out here as well as she'd hoped, though, and until the arrival of a lone stranger just yesterday, Vicky had been utterly alone for days, wondering how she would possibly survive on her own and with nothing.

She knew the silence would be back to haunt her as she stood watching Eric Branson jog up the gravel road until he was lost from her view, the sounds of his boots shuffling in loose rocks finally fading away in the distance. When he'd arrived, Vicky had no idea who he was, and she was afraid he would kill her or worse if he saw her. Fortunately, she'd been near the barn the afternoon before when she first spotted him out among the pines between the ruins of the house and the road. She had ducked inside and watched through a knothole in the weathered siding as he approached, noting that he was very careful, stopping often to look and listen, as if he were expecting to run into an ambush or something. He looked ready for it if he did too, sweeping the area before him with the muzzle of a menacing weapon Vicky knew was some kind of machine gun. It was normal though for people of both the good and the bad sort to go about armed these days; anything less was simply foolish in such dangerous times. Knowing that, she understood that the man's cautious approach did not necessarily make him a bad guy, but she knew too that present circumstances made most everyone an opportunist. Survival demanded it, and she figured he'd seen the driveway leading in from the road and decided to come and see if there was anything of use to be found here.

Vicky hoped the man would go away when he saw that the house had been burned, but that discovery only seemed to pique his curiosity. After snooping around the blackened rubble, he spotted the two graves in what had been her grandparents' backyard. Vicky had found it difficult to dig into the hard, rocky ground there, and in fact the bodies were only partially buried. After doing the best she could, she'd worked for hours covering them with the largest stones she could gather and carry from nearby, piling them on until she was exhausted. She hoped her efforts would dissuade the carnivorous scavengers that she knew were around.

The stranger crouched near the two rock piles as if to study them, but they didn't hold his attention for long. The barn was the only structure still standing on the place, so Vicky wasn't surprised that he turned his attention to it next. She wanted to run but doing so would put her out in the open before she could reach the surrounding forest. The man would see her, and she'd be an easy target for his rifle if he chose to shoot. She also considered climbing up into the loft, but she already knew there was no good place to hide up there and she would be cornered if he went up to investigate, which he probably would if he entered the barn at all. She opted instead for the pile of loose hay where she'd been sleeping near the back entrance, digging her way into it and curling into a ball before gathering more of it over her body like a blanket. She barely had time to settle in and quiet her breathing before she heard the man walk inside and stop, no doubt scanning the dark interior for any sign of life. Her heart pounded as he passed close to the hay pile. *Was she really completely covered? Did he already know she was in there?*

But when he turned away and she heard him climb the creaky ladder to the loft, she knew she'd made the right decision. He would have found her up there for sure, and she wasn't taking any chances that he might still discover her in the hay when he came back down. She decided to make a run for it while he was up there out of sight, and she would have gotten away with it too, if she hadn't accidentally knocked over a stupid board leaning against the wall, making a huge racket that betrayed her presence.

Vicky heard the man jump to the ground as she bolted, and she fully expected to feel his bullets rip through her back as she sprinted for the nearby trees. But instead, she'd been stopped in her tracks by the single word he shouted: *MEGAN! This stranger had called her by her best friend's name! Somehow, he thought she was Megan, but how did he even know Megan?* She turned around to face him so that he could see that she wasn't, and then in the following moments of confusion, it sunk in that he was telling her he was Megan's dad! When he said his name was Eric Branson, Vicky had to believe him. He completely fit the description of the man Megan told her about—old enough to be her dad but lean, fit and dangerous—a Special Forces soldier who had spent his career fighting wars all over the world.

Megan seldom saw him, but she'd said he might come back to the U.S. now that there was a war to fight at home. She didn't think he would come because of her, but now Eric Branson was telling Vicky otherwise. Megan *was* the reason he was back, and he'd crossed half the continent with great difficulty to get to Colorado, where he'd hoped to finally find her. Vicky hated to be the one to disappoint him, but she had to tell him the truth of what little she knew of Megan's whereabouts. Her father's search unfortunately wasn't going to end here at her grandpa's ranch, no matter how much he'd hoped it would be so. That was when Vicky learned from him that Megan's mother was involved too, and that Eric had found a note from her stating that she and their friend Jonathan had headed here before him. The two of them had left Boulder based on information that Megan had fled the university campus with some of her friends, one of whom had grandparents living on this remote mountain ranch. Vicky told Eric that was her, and that they *had* all come here, but not before a lot of other things happened first. And then a lot more had happened since. Megan had left before the worst of it, and Vicky had no way of knowing how far along on her journey she was. Vicky told him she was the only one remaining here and that the two graves he'd noticed contained the remains of her grandparents.

She told Eric she'd had no idea what she was going to do next or how she was going to survive before he showed up. The barn was the only shelter still standing on the property, and though it didn't block all the cold wind that swept down the valley, it kept her out of the open and sleeping in the hay provided enough insulation to keep her from freezing to death at night. She had little left to eat, however, and she'd known for days that if her luck didn't change, she was going to starve if she didn't figure something out. But Eric's arrival *did* change her luck. He'd given her food, sharing his rations with her, and he'd made her a promise that he would take her with him when he continued his search for Megan.

But before that could happen, she would have to be alone again for at least a couple of days, and she didn't like it one bit. Eric had insisted on going back to a remote homestead where he'd spotted some horses on his way there, and she was in no position to argue. She was too weak to keep up with him crossing the mountains on foot, even at a slow walking pace, and Eric wasn't going to settle for slow, knowing his daughter was so far ahead of him and heading to New Mexico on horseback. He said they would need horses as well if they were ever going to catch up, although seeing him head out at the pace he set when he left that morning, Vicky wasn't sure. She thought maybe he could do it on foot if he weren't burdened by her, but she was grateful that he'd offered to take her. Going with him was really her only choice if she didn't want to die here alone, and it was scary enough to let him leave at all, even though she knew he had to try and find horses. He'd promised to return as soon as possible, and he'd left her some of his food as well as his Glock pistol to give her some comfort while he was away.

As she thought about what Eric had told her about his journey to get here, and all the obstacles he encountered and overcame, Vicky couldn't help but think how different things might have been had he only arrived a little sooner. If he'd gotten here before Megan and Aaron left, they wouldn't have to go looking for them at all. And if he'd been here when those other men came, her grandparents might be alive now and their house still standing. Eric would have stopped those killers. Everything Megan had told her about him was evident at a glance when she saw him in person. He had a friendly smile for her, but there was a faraway look in his eyes and something else in them too that told her he wasn't the sort of man one would want for an enemy. She wouldn't be afraid as long as she was with him, no matter where they went, but the return of that awful silence in his absence now put her nerves back on edge, and doubts began to creep into her mind.

What if Eric didn't come back? Now that he knew which way Megan went, did he really need her along, slowing him down? It wasn't like Vicky could show him the way, because she'd never been farther south in these mountains than this ranch and she'd already told him all she knew of Megan's plans and proposed route. Why should he go out of his way to try and find horses for the two of them when he could already be well on his way after Megan without them? Had he already circled back after he was out of sight of the barn and picked up her trail even now? Couldn't those Special Forces guys like him run all day without stopping? Vicky couldn't quit thinking of the possibilities. So many people had betrayed her and let her down since society began to unravel that it was what she'd come to expect. Why should Megan's dad, a man she'd never met before today, be any different? He didn't owe her a thing, and after all, he'd let Megan and her mom down too, time and time again, according to what Megan had told her. The man had chosen a life that kept him away from his family, and as a result, Megan scarcely knew him herself. *Did he come here now only because he felt guilty about all that and was trying to make up for it?* Vicky didn't know, and she sure didn't know how *she* fit into his plans, if she really did at all.

She hated feeling so much mistrust so soon after he left, because she really wanted to believe in him. But she couldn't quiet the inner voices in her head, not here in this utter silence, where those voices were the strongest signals reaching her brain. She was aware that the voices were playing tricks on her, and that she'd been traumatized by the recent events she'd experienced but understanding that didn't help. She couldn't shut it off while sitting there waiting, doing nothing in that barn, so she decided to try walking around outside for a bit, in hopes of finding something to distract her and get her mind off her fears. And having Eric's Glock gave her the confidence to do so. While her experience with firearms was only basic, she did know how to aim and shoot a pistol. Her grandfather had taught her with his Colt .45, which he said was just like the one he carried when he was in the Army. When Vicky mentioned this to Eric, he said the Glock wasn't much different, and actually a little easier to use, as it had less recoil and no safety mechanisms to get confused with. He also said it was ready to go with a round already in the chamber and a full magazine with 15 more just like the first. A small Kydex trigger guard that Eric used for carrying it inside his waistband would prevent accidental discharges. He showed her how to yank it off by the belt loop cord attached to it and assured her that the pistol couldn't fire as long as the trigger was covered and couldn't be pulled. Vicky hoped she wouldn't need it but having the gun in hand definitely made her feel better. She knew she should have more faith in Eric simply because he left it with her, but trust was just so hard now.

She scanned the open pastures and pine-covered slopes surrounding the barn to make sure she was still alone once outside, and then she made her way towards the ruins of the house. Eric had piled more stones onto the two graves to complete the job she'd started and then that evening while they were talking in the barn, he'd inscribed their names on a weathered board that the two of them placed at the head of the graves. Vicky paused to stare at it for a moment before walking by, grateful for what Eric had done, and then she went on past the house rubble and made her way to the front gate, where she stood and looked down the gravel lane to the road. She wasn't expecting to see or hear anything out there, but her anxiety drew her to the entrance anyway.

As she stood looking for nothing in particular, Vicky longed to hear *anything* that might break the silence. The call of a small bird or the sound of a squirrel scampering through the pines would make her feel better, but if there were any small creatures nearby, they weren't moving now. It was as if she were truly the only living thing left on the property. Vicky leaned back against the rough bark of a tree as gathering clouds of dark thoughts swirled around her. She knew that even if Eric returned tomorrow, the earliest she could reasonably expect him, the hours in between were going to drag like days and her time alone would seem like forever. She didn't know how to deal with that other than breaking up the wait by moving around a bit. She would sit out here as long as she could stand it, and then find another spot to wait some more. Settling on the ground at the base of the tree trunk, she passed at least a full hour before her legs felt stiff and she had to get up and shake it out. She was about to turn back for the short walk to the barn when a gut feeling suddenly overcame her; a feeling that maybe she *was* no longer alone.

She felt her heart began to race as she scanned her surroundings with a growing sense of panic. A moment later a sound reached her ears, confirming that she wasn't just imagining things. *Someone was out there on the road!* Vicky did her best to keep her breathing in control as she listened carefully, trying to figure it out. And then it dawned on her that the sound that broke the silence was the sound of approaching horses, but not coming from the direction in which Eric went, which was east to where the road eventually dead-ended at a trailhead. *No, these horses were coming from the west, following the one road that led in to connect the ranch to the rest of the world.* Vicky could clearly hear their hooves crunching the gravel now, and she could hear barely audible voices as the riders conversed. She didn't know how many there were, but there was certainly more than one, so it wasn't Eric Branson. And she knew that even if there weren't more than one and they weren't coming from the wrong direction, Eric couldn't have possibly found horses and made it back here with them so soon, as he'd only been gone a few hours.

Vicky quickly considered her options as she looked around for the best place to hide close at hand. There wasn't time to run back to the barn before whoever was riding those horses came into view if they turned into the drive, and besides, being the only structure still standing there, the barn would be a magnet to them as it had been to Eric. Vicky couldn't risk it again. Her top priority was to stay out of sight until the approaching riders left, and that meant she had to disappear from view *right now*. She slipped through the trees some 200 feet to the east of the driveway to a small outcrop of jagged rock that would provide concealment as long as the strangers didn't approach it directly. By the time she had settled in behind it, lying flat on her stomach in a position where she could watch the entrance, the riders were in view, heading straight onto the property just as she'd feared they would.

Vicky had Eric's Glock in her hand as she propped herself up on her elbows just enough to see over the rocks. For all she knew, the approaching strangers were friends of her grandparents, finally making their way here to check on them. But until she knew, she had to assume everyone she encountered was a threat. That was the world she now found herself in, whether she liked living that way or not. Her actions yesterday would have failed her for certain if the man who found her in the barn had been one of the bad ones. Vicky was determined not to make another such mistake, and as the approaching horses and riders drew close enough that she finally got a good look at them, she was glad she was well hidden. One of the three horses was unmistakably a gelding named Tucker that had been her grandpa's favorite. The other two were Appaloosas as well that she recognized from the ranch, and seeing them together, she knew exactly who had taken them and who was riding them now. The three thieves in the saddles weren't strangers at all, but rather her former friends that had stolen those horses as well as all the supplies they could carry when they set off from the ranch in pursuit of Megan and Aaron. Vicky's grip tightened on the Glock as she stared at the rider on Tucker's back in disgust. *What in the hell was Gareth Mabry up to now? Why would he and Jeremy and Brett come back here after what they'd done? And where was Colleen? Why wasn't she with them?"*

TWO

VICKY WATCHED AS GARETH AND HIS TWO companions reined in their stolen horses at the sight of the burned-down ranch house. She was pretty sure they weren't expecting to find this, as they had taken the horses and left several days before the men who'd attacked the place arrived. She assumed they were back here because they wanted something, maybe just a place to go after running into no telling what out there in the mountains. She also thought it was safe to assume that they hadn't found Megan and Aaron, or if they had, they hadn't been able to persuade Megan to return with them. Colleen's absence was more puzzling though. She and Brett had been mostly inseparable since they'd first hooked up. Unless Colleen was waiting behind somewhere nearby, Vicky thought it likely something must have happened to prevent her returning with him.

Regardless of why the three were back, Vicky had no use for any of them after what they'd done. Megan had made a good decision to get away from Gareth while she still could, and Vicky could only hope he'd indeed been unsuccessful in his attempts to track her down. She hoped too that they would simply turn around and leave when they saw that there was nothing left of the house but burned-out rubble, but of course, they didn't. Instead, Gareth dismounted and pulled the rifle that had also belonged to her grandpa out of its saddle scabbard, handing his reins to Jeremy before walking over to the house site to investigate. As he kicked around in the rubble, probably hoping to find something still useable, the other two got down and tied off the horses to the hitching post that was still out front, so they could join him. Vicky was furious as she watched them. They had no right to be here, but she didn't dare confront them, outnumbered as she was. Eric Branson could have handled the situation if he were still here, and no doubt would convince them to leave, but she didn't dare try. The best she could do was stay out of sight behind the rocks and hope they would move on. With all of them dismounted though, she doubted they planned on leaving right away, at least not until they had investigated the barn.

Vicky cringed as she watched Gareth walk directly to the two graves as soon as he noticed them. She heard him call out something to the other two about how it was the "old man" and the "old woman". *Yeah, that's right!* Vicky thought, *the very same 'old man' and 'old woman' who took you jerks in and gave you food and a place to stay before you left with all that you stole from them!* Vicky watched him drop to a knee between the graves, studying them closely. Eric had piled on enough extra rocks that the bodies were now well covered from view. *If Gareth and his friends started moving some of those stones away though...* Vicky tightened her grip on the Glock. It wasn't aimed directly at any of her three former acquaintances, but she wouldn't hesitate to take on all three of them before she watched them desecrate her grandparents' graves.

But thankfully, it didn't come to that. Gareth seemed to lose interest in the graves, but she heard her own name come up in the exchange of conversation as Brett and Jeremy made their way around the ruins of the house to join him. Vicky was sure they were wondering where she was, knowing she had still been here with her grandparents after they left in pursuit of Megan. They had to be wondering exactly what had happened here and where she was now. *Someone* had dug those graves and moved all those stones, so they likely suspected she'd survived. The barn was the only shelter left, so naturally, they would search it for any sign she'd been in there, and Vicky knew that they would find the wrappers from the MREs she'd shared with Eric, as well as the unopened ones he'd left with her. Now she would go hungry tonight, regardless of whether the three hung around or left when they didn't find her. Vicky didn't know what she could do about it though. She eyed the horses and considered how long it would take to get up and sprint to the hitching post, mount Tucker and ride off. Tucker knew her, and she'd ridden him many times, so she knew she could trust him, but no matter how fast she might be able to gallop away on him, she would be an easy target for a rifle, and Gareth would shoot too—Vicky knew he would—because without the horses they would be stranded.

The idea of taking back her grandpa's horses appealed to her because of the principle of it most of all. The horses, saddles and some of the guns the three were carrying all belonged to her grandpa, and it burned her up to think of how they'd betrayed him and taken them. While it would be easier for her if they just rode away after looking around, Vicky considered too that Eric might return tomorrow or the day after empty-handed, unable to find horses they could use to go after Megan and Aaron. If she could steal back these three, they could serve as a backup, but if she did that now, she couldn't wait here for Eric to return, so that was a problem too. These were the thoughts she weighed as she watched Gareth and his friends walk to the barn. She was *so* tempted, but she wasn't sure if she could realistically pull something like that off. If there was going to be a chance at all though, she knew it might come in the next few minutes, when the three of them were inside the barn and out of sight. The window of opportunity would be brief though, she was sure, because there wasn't much they'd find to keep the three of them in there for long.

Vicky didn't get the opportunity to see if she could actually summon the courage to make such a bold move though, at least not then. Just as he reached the barn entrance, she saw Gareth stop and look out across the far pasture while saying something to the others. Then Jeremy turned and started back to where they'd left the horses. Gareth had sent him back to get something while he and Brett went inside the barn. Vicky was still stuck and unable to make a move, and she was getting impatient, wondering what they were going to do next and how long they might hang around.

By the time Jeremy made it back to them, Gareth and Brett were outside again. Gareth had two green packages in his hands; the two remaining MREs that Eric had given Vicky. With those and the trash from the opened one, they had hard evidence that someone was around, and Vicky figured they would think it was her, because who else would bother to bury her dead grandparents? Gareth took the binoculars Jeremy brought him from his saddlebags and used them to carefully scan the surrounding pastures and wooded slopes. Would they go out looking for her now? Vicky didn't know, but their trip back here had proven fruitless as far as finding supplies or anything else they could steal. They might think she had more food hidden away somewhere, or they might think anything she had wasn't worth the effort. Still, Vicky would never trust Gareth again. She knew what he was capable of, despite how nice he may have seemed in the beginning.

It wasn't a mystery why Megan fell for the guy back then. Gareth Mabry was good-looking, outgoing and friendly and seemed to take a keen interest in the people he met. It was rare to find a guy that would listen, but Gareth did, and Megan found that to be his most charming virtue. When he came over to their place or Vicky went out with them somewhere, he listened to her too, and she had to admit it occasionally made her a bit jealous of her roommate. Vicky was doing her best to focus on her classes at the time, having been through a bad breakup with the guy she'd thought she was in love with just the semester before. She was happy for Megan, but she still sometimes wished she had someone that paid that kind of attention to her, and what girl wouldn't?

The events that began taking place earlier that spring semester, however, revealed another side of Gareth. He quickly lost interest in things academic and shifted his focus to politics and activism, not just watching, but getting personally involved. Wherever there was a protest or similar gathering, Gareth was there. He wanted to participate, and he was convinced that it would make a difference. Vicky and Megan wanted no part of that stuff and just hoped things would settle down to normal again, but by then, Megan was in deep with Gareth and was going along enough to keep his interest. Neither Megan nor Vicky believed anything *they* could do would stop the terror attacks, but many students did.

They blamed the actions of the government for it rather than the terrorists themselves, and they were convinced that if enough of them made themselves heard, those actions would be changed or stopped. When that didn't seem to work, they got louder, but when words clearly weren't enough, they started to break and burn things. This wasn't just at their particular campus, of course—it was happening all over—and it intensified as the weeks went by and the semester was drawing to a close. It went far beyond the universities and student protesters though. Organized anarchist and anti-government groups that had been preparing and waiting for just the right circumstances to act seized on the opportunities created by this growing chaos. Their indiscriminate acts of infrastructure sabotage left citizens on both sides of the argument cut off from power, communications and the delivery of essential supplies. People died as an indirect result of these actions and then more died as the authorities responded and the use of force escalated.

Vicky had watched as Gareth became more excited about these developments and she listened as he defended the position of the insurrectionists, saying that it was time for a regime change and time to get rid of the old, corrupt system and help bring about a new one that would be fair for all. Gareth wanted to be a part of this change, and he wanted Megan there with him. Vicky remembered the long, heated discussions they'd had in the apartment, but Megan was infatuated with him despite their disagreements. At the time, things hadn't turned truly violent there in Boulder just yet. There was some arson and property destruction, and lots of arrests when the police in riot gear responded, but so far no one had been seriously injured. The worst then was that the normal functions of the university ground to a halt, and just at the time final exams would normally be taking place. Even then, Vicky thought it was futile to hang around and she'd already suggested to Megan that maybe they should leave and go to her grandparents' ranch. But Megan wasn't going anywhere without Gareth, and he wouldn't hear of leaving.

"If we back down now, nothing will ever change. Running away will just let them win!"

"They're going to win anyway, Gareth. They always do. No one can overthrow the government, not here, in the most powerful nation on the planet!"

"All governments fall eventually, Vicky! History proves it! This one isn't immune. None of them are."

"Maybe so, but how many people have to die for something like that to happen? Do you want to die for it? I know I don't! Megan can certainly tell you what you'd be up against if you try. Right or wrong, her dad has been fighting wars for this country her entire life. He's somewhere in Europe now, and you know how bad it's been there. Do you really want things to get like that here?"

Gareth was smart enough to know all this, but he didn't let that stop him. Megan was smart enough too, but lately, she wasn't exactly proud of what her dad had been doing, even if she did know very little of the actual

21

details of his work. When she was younger, she had thought it was pretty cool that he was a Navy SEAL, and she'd looked up to that. He was a hero to her then, fighting to rescue people and help those who just wanted to have the freedoms everyone dreamed of. But he'd left regular military service years ago, and now worked as a private contractor, supposedly for better pay and so he could be home more. She didn't know about the pay, but the being home part certainly didn't happen. Her mom *said* he wasn't a mercenary, but Megan knew better. Combat was the one thing her dad was truly good at, and she doubted he was merely working in a supporting role, and she wondered if he was even one of the good guys anymore. Megan had told Vicky many times that she didn't know. She said the more she learned about what was actually going on in the world, the more she doubted everything she'd ever believed in. Vicky had her own doubts, but no one in her family was in the military now, fighting in those wars, and so she could only imagine how Megan must feel. Vicky's grandpa had been in the Army as a young man, but that was after World War Two, so he'd never seen actual combat.

Gareth said that because the military was spread so thin all over the globe fighting wars in countries where they had no business, this was the perfect time for revolution to happen at home. He believed that once it gained enough momentum, it would be unstoppable, and as things worsened with the beginning of summer, it seemed that he might be right. Vicky still didn't know for sure, but she suspected that Gareth was involved in the sabotage attack on the local power grid that eventually led to the shutdown and occupation of the Boulder campus and opening of the detainment center there where many of their former fellow students were still locked up, as far as she knew. Gareth had told Megan he was going to be away camping for a few days, and she and Vicky both knew it wasn't just about backpacking or chilling out in the mountains. While he was gone, there were explosions that took out two major substations, leaving the city without power, and then more fires that started during the resultant blackout. The shooting started the second night, close enough that Vicky and Megan could hear it from where they were hunkered down in their apartment. They didn't see Gareth until the day after that, when he came back to tell Megan they had to get out of town. National Guard troops were moving into the area to back up the police and sheriff departments, and the rumors were flying regarding their intentions. Gareth said they all needed to relocate to a campsite in the mountains nearby, where many of the members of the resistance were already gathered.

After much discussion and more arguing back and forth, Vicky and Megan agreed to go with him. Camping out seemed preferable to staying in an apartment with no electricity and no Internet or cell service. The last two had stopped working only the day before Gareth returned, and he claimed the authorities had shut down the signals to prevent the resistance from organizing more actions. This was believable, because they'd already heard reports of this happening in other areas where direct action had started sooner. It made sense for them to do this, because they still had their radios and other secure means of communication and cutting off communication among ordinary citizens made them easier to divide and control. Gareth said the power wouldn't be coming on again anytime soon either. Even once the damage was repaired, the authorities would keep the grid down deliberately in most areas while working to bring the people into submission. Vicky *knew* there had to be a lot more that Gareth was leaving out though, and she found out she was right when they reached the camp where this "resistance" movement was gathering.

The first thing that surprised her was seeing all the firearms that were in evidence. Gareth hadn't told them about that, and when Megan asked, he said being armed was necessary because it was the police who were escalating the violence and they already had weapons and were willing to use them. But despite what he said, it didn't take Vicky and Megan long to figure out that mere self-defense wasn't the motivation here. The group camped in the mountains was made up of a mix of male and female students of college age, but there were many older men among them as well. Vicky didn't know whether the latter were locals or outsiders who had arrived from elsewhere, but many of them were very vocal and intense, taking charge each night around the big central campfire with rallying speeches that whipped the rest of the group into a frenzy. To Vicky, it brought to mind old Western movies she'd watched with her grandpa; scenes of fierce Indian warriors dancing around a bonfire in preparation to go on the warpath. It made her uncomfortable, because she didn't believe more violence was going to solve anything. She didn't like some of the things she'd heard the police and other authority figures were doing, but that didn't mean they deserved to be shot. Self-defense was one thing, but what these people were stirring up and advocating was armed revolution, and whether it was part of the bigger movement elsewhere or not, it essentially amounted to a declaration of war.

At the time, she'd felt stuck there with few other options. Getting back home to her parents' house in Portland seemed impossible, and Megan's family was even farther away in south Florida. Getting enough gas to make a trip to either place was out of the question, as it was already in short supply even before the loss of power forced the remaining service stations to close. They'd also heard about roadblocks and checkpoints that were being set up on the highways, and Gareth said he'd personally seen some of those just outside the city. No one knew who could pass through them and who could not, but attempting it wasn't worth the risk of getting arrested and locked up, especially so soon after the explosions that were being blamed on practically the entire student body at the university. The only real option to travel without being hassled was the network of biking and hiking trails that connected the city with the recreation and wilderness areas of the surrounding mountains. That was how they reached the camp to begin with, but they weren't really prepared to travel on foot for any distance. Vicky enjoyed hiking, but she'd never done it with a heavy load of gear and supplies, and certainly not alone.

Even before they'd left their apartment near the campus though, she'd thought of her grandparents' ranch, and how it would surely be a safe refuge, if only they could somehow get there. She'd mentioned it to Megan and Gareth, but he shot down that idea immediately, saying it was stupid to go off and hide in the middle of nowhere when they were on the cusp of making a real difference here. Vicky was convinced then that he was crazy and dangerous, and that if he continued on that path he'd be arrested or killed. Gareth had to learn that the hard way though, and he did when he and several of the guys from the gathering set up a roadblock of their own to ambush a convoy of trucks bringing supplies and equipment to the now police-occupied campus.

They mostly succeeded with their plan, stopping the trucks on a remote stretch of highway bordered by steep wooded slopes. But the ensuing shootout left all of the truck drivers and their armed guards wounded or dead, as well as three attackers from the camp. One of those who died made it back to the camp with assistance from the others but had lost so much blood that he died there in front of them all when they couldn't save him. The squeamish among them lost some of their will to fight right there, but the trucks in the convoy had indeed been loaded with supplies, and the surviving raiders had hauled all they could carry with them when they fled. Unfortunately, when they went back to get the rest of it, they found it impossible. It was assumed that someone from the convoy had managed to call for help in the thick of the shooting. From the crest of a high ridge overlooking the road, the returning raiders saw that more trucks full of armed men had arrived at the scene of the attack. Worst of all, they had dogs with them and appeared to be readying to track down whoever was responsible for the ambush. From that moment forward, the mountain campsite was no longer a safe base of operations, and those that had been staying there had little choice but to disperse and try to evade capture. Many were unsuccessful, including some of their friends. Vicky now knew that one of those, a girl named Jena Adams, was among those who'd been rounded up. She learned this when Eric showed her the letter from Megan's mom that led him here to the ranch. Jena was the one who'd told Shauna about the ranch and their plans to go there. She knew where it was because Vicky and Megan had tried to get her to come with them when they made their escape. Jena didn't though, but now at least Vicky knew she was alive. Some of the others from the camp likely weren't so lucky, based on the amount of gunfire they'd heard as their small group struck out into the wilderness to the south just in time.

Gareth had reluctantly agreed to come with them, and Brett, Jeremy, Colleen and a guy named Aaron made up the rest of their party. Aaron knew the mountains better than any of them, and with his guidance, they finally made their way to the ranch after many long days of hiking with far too little to eat. All of them survived it, and Vicky's grandparents welcomed them in. A lot had changed on that hike though--especially between Megan and Gareth. By the time they'd arrived there, the two of them were no longer a couple, but Gareth didn't seem bothered by it at first. He was too busy getting on the good side of Vicky's grandpa, smooth-talking him just the way he had Megan, in order to gain whatever advantage he could. Vicky thought back on some of the bullshit he'd told the good-hearted old man and seethed with anger as she lay there hiding behind the rocks. It was so unfair that that bastard was still alive, while under those stones lay two of the best people she'd ever known. And to add to the injustice, Gareth and his buddies had the nerve to come back here to his land, riding his stolen horses!

She watched as Gareth tore open the MRE's and divided up the contents with his buddies. She thought they might leave when they were finished eating the only food she had, but then Brett filled a bucket he'd found in the barn from the hand pump at the well, and they carried water and hay out to the horses. When they removed their saddles and took them into the barn, Vicky knew they intended to spend at least one night there, and now she was not only deprived of her lunch and dinner, but cut-off from her only shelter and facing a night outside in the freezing cold. Vicky was furious, and more determined than ever to figure out a way to make those jerks regret ever coming back.

THREE

As she watched and waited, Vicky thought it would be a lot easier to take back the stolen horses after dark if Gareth and his companions left them tied up outside the barn, which it appeared they planned to do. But a quick getaway into the night would be risky for all sorts of reasons, not to mention how cold it would be after sundown. If she were going to be faced with a night spent outdoors, Vicky knew she needed to reach a somewhat sheltered location while there was still light. It might be prudent to just leave now and walk, but she *wanted* those horses—not just because they'd belonged to her grandpa—but because she didn't want Gareth and his two fellow thieves to get away with what they'd done. She wanted to leave them stranded on foot with nothing because that's exactly what they deserved. Even if they spent the night, Vicky knew they might still leave first thing in the morning, long before Eric returned. She didn't want to take a chance on letting them get away with the horses again, so she decided it was worth watching and waiting some more, just in case an opportunity presented itself.

The rock outcrop gave her a good vantage point from which to do so, but the waiting was tedious. Gareth, Jeremy and Brett did little other than moving their saddlebags inside the barn from late morning to early afternoon. They seemed to be talking constantly, but their voices were too low and too far away for Vicky to hear anything they were saying. She knew they must be disappointed with what they'd found here and were probably discussing what they would do next. The old barn offered them little in the way of long-term accommodations. It was a marginal shelter at best, and completely insufficient for the much colder weather that would be coming soon when winter actually arrived, a problem Vicky had been all too aware of before Eric showed up. She would have been forced to take her chances by moving on, even if she'd had food, unless she began work immediately to gather sufficient firewood and attempt to improve the barn for the weather that would come.

She was about to give up on any chance of making a move before dark when finally, around mid-afternoon, Gareth and Jeremy set off on foot across the pasture with their guns, leaving Brett behind to watch the horses and other stuff. Vicky guessed that they were either going out to look for signs of her, or perhaps to try their luck at hunting. Gareth had taken to hunting with enthusiasm shortly after they'd all arrived there in the summer, having already gotten a taste of it on the trek there. Aaron was the only one of their group who had prior hunting experience, and when Gareth expressed interest, he'd begun teaching him along the way. They'd had little success while on the move, and Aaron said that was to be expected, but once they'd arrived at the ranch that changed. Vicky's grandpa knew where the game was in the surrounding mountains, and since he already knew how to shoot well enough, even Gareth was soon contributing to the larder. Knowing how to hunt was a useful skill to have now, of course, especially in a place teeming with deer and other game, and Vicky figured that what Gareth had learned of it was helping them get by. It made sense they would try their luck here today, especially since he knew where to look in the vicinity of the ranch. But regardless of where they were going and why, seeing two of them disappear into the trees on the far side of the pasture gave Vicky hope. It would be much easier to steal back those horses from one of them than from all three, and she made up her mind to do just that before Gareth and Jeremy had time to return.

Of the three of them, Brett was the one Vicky knew least well. He'd been so wrapped up with Colleen most of the time that she and Megan hadn't talked with either of them much, even during the long trek from Boulder. Colleen, they already knew from classes they had with her, but she'd met Brett more recently at one of the protest events right before classes got canceled. Unlike Gareth, he seemed to be the quiet type, and tended to keep whatever he was thinking to himself, or at least between himself and Colleen. As Vicky watched him now, she wondered again what could have happened that she wasn't with him here today. From the way those two stuck together, it seemed unlikely they'd willingly be apart for any length of time, but at least with her gone Vicky didn't have to worry about getting the drop on two of them.

She knew for certain what Gareth was capable of, because she'd already seen it. He wouldn't hesitate to stop her from taking those horses by any means necessary, even if it meant shooting her dead. Whether Brett was as dangerous, Vicky didn't know, but she had to assume so anyway and take no chances. She considered trying to sneak closer when his back was turned so she would be ready to quickly grab the horses if he happened to step back into the barn. If he were unarmed, she could probably pull that off, since she was confident the animals would recognize her and not panic when she approached them. Her riding skills were good enough for a quick getaway, even bareback, but the problem was that Brett *was* armed, and Vicky couldn't ride fast enough to get out of rifle range if he happened to hear her or look her way at the wrong moment. It was simply too risky, so she decided the best way to do this was to disarm him first. While that was risky too, the odds were far better now that it was one-on-one. She was aware her window of opportunity might be short, though. Gareth and Jeremy's hunt might turn into nothing more than a short stroll in the woods, and Vicky couldn't afford to wait and see. Besides, she needed time to put some distance between herself and all three of them, so she could find a place to hole up and survive the night without fear of being found. She would have to come back tomorrow to try and meet Eric but figuring that out would come later. For now, her focus was narrowed to Brett and the three horses.

Vicky could tell Brett was bored from the way he acted as she watched him. He sat for a while and then he stood and paced, mostly looking at the ground and seemingly lost in his thoughts, probably thoughts of Colleen, Vicky figured. She decided that rather than try and sneak up on him, she would simply walk up as if nothing had happened and she totally expected to find him here. While that would startle him, she doubted he would shoot her on sight or anything like that. And if he freaked out and yelled for Gareth and Jeremy, they were too far away now to hear him. Even if her appearance resulted in gunfire being exchanged, they were too far away to get back in time to stop her from riding away with those horses. Her mind made up, Vicky stood and tucked the Glock into the waistband of her jeans so that it was hidden in the small of her back, and then she boldly left the rock outcrop and walked deliberately through the pine grove straight in the direction of the barn. She kept her focus on Brett as she walked, and even though she was in plain view if he'd bothered to look up, he didn't. When she was about 40 feet away, she decided she'd better stop and get his attention:

"Brett?"

When Brett heard her voice and looked up to see her standing so close, he nearly lost his balance as he turned towards her and fumbled with his rifle in surprise.

"DON'T SHOOT BRETT! It's me. Vicky!"

"Vicky? What are you doing here? We didn't think there was anyone around! We didn't even know if you were still alive or not!" Brett glanced over at the two rocky graves as he said this.

"My grandma and grandpa are not. But I'm still here. It looks like you found the last of my food though and helped yourself!" Vicky nodded at the MRE wrappers on the ground.

"Sorry. We didn't know those rations were yours. We figured some military assholes must have left them here."

"What do you mean, 'we'? Who's with you, Brett?" Vicky pretended not to know. "Colleen?"

Brett looked at her with a blank stare before responding. "Gareth and Jeremy are with me. They're hunting but they'll be back soon. I don't know where Colleen is. She went missing when we were out there in the mountains. We'd lost all our food crossing a stream. The pack-horse carrying everything we had slipped on the rocks and got swept downstream in the rapids to a waterfall. We couldn't find a way down there to get it, so we set up camp not far from there and went hunting for something to eat. Colleen stayed behind with the other horses and when we came back that afternoon, she was just *gone!* Her horse was gone too. We looked for her all the next day, but never saw anything. I wanted to keep looking, but Gareth said there was no use and insisted we keep going. We did go on for a few more days, but the hunting wasn't any good where we were, and we never could really find enough to eat. It looked like we would starve if we kept on, so we came back here, because by then Gareth said there was no way Megan and Aaron could have made it all that way either, and that they were probably both dead."

"So, you came back here to see what else you could steal...." Vicky glared at him, after glancing at the three tethered horses.

"We didn't really 'steal' those horses from your grandpa, Vicky. We just borrowed them so Gareth could try to catch up to Megan. We were always planning on bringing them back. I'm just sorry he's not here so we could explain that to him. What happened to him and your grandma anyway?"

"It doesn't concern you," Vicky said, reaching behind her and drawing the Glock. Before Brett realized what she was doing, she had leveled it at his face, and had subtly closed the gap by several more steps, making certain she was close enough that she would not miss if she had to shoot. "Drop to your knees and put that rifle on the ground nice and easy! That belonged to my grandpa too, and you'd better be gentle with it!"

"But Vicky! We're friends! There's no need to point a gun at me!"

"Do it, Brett! I *will* shoot you if you don't! I swear I will!"

Brett followed her instructions this time, though the puzzled look on his face told her he was still surprised that she would point a gun at him. Vicky was dumbfounded to realize that this idiot really didn't see that he'd done anything wrong. He was just like Gareth and Jeremy.

"Now crawl backward away from that rifle on your knees and keep your hands where I can see them. If you try anything, I'll shoot you, Brett. I'm serious!"

"I'm not trying anything! I just don't understand what you want!"

"I want you to stay down there where you are, that's what I want! I'm going to take my grandpa's horses and leave. You three had better do the same when Gareth and Jeremy get back. I have a friend looking out for me now, and let me tell you, he is one badass dude. He'll be back soon, and if he finds you here, you're going to wish you'd never set foot on this ranch!"

"You can't take those horses now, Vicky! We'll have no way to get around! What will we do?"

"You'll walk, I guess! And be glad you still can! I should shoot you anyway just on principle! Grandpa said stealing a man's horse was a capital offense out here in these parts not so long ago and said that's what all of you deserved when he discovered what you'd done. The way things are going now, Brett, those old ways are coming back into fashion. You should know that by now, you dumbass!"

Vicky picked up the rifle from the ground while keeping the pistol pointed at Brett. She was keeping a tough facade, but she was truly glad that he was being compliant. She hadn't had to shoot anyone yet since all this mess started, and she hoped she would never have to, especially not another college student her age that she actually knew by name. She backed away to create some distance, but she was confident Brett wasn't going to try anything now after surrendering the rifle so easily.

The old bolt-action Remington was one she'd shot with her grandpa many times during her summer vacations. It was a .22 Magnum small game and varmint gun that he always kept handy by the front door of the house, using it more for plinking than anything else. She was glad to get it back, but she wanted the other guns that Gareth and Jeremy had taken too—her grandpa's deer rifle and shotgun that he'd so generously loaned them when they'd all arrived here. She knew that retrieving them wasn't likely to happen though, and she felt lucky to have just the one rifle and the opportunity to leave with the horses.

"You need to wait until Gareth and Jeremy come back," Brett said. "Don't just take the horses and leave us like this. They will want to work something out, I promise you. We should all stick together like before to survive. You should know that is a better idea!"

"Bringing any of you here was a *bad* idea!" Vicky said. "All three of you betrayed my trust and betrayed my family and your other friends, including Megan. There's nothing to work out. I just want all of you *gone* when I come back, and I *will* be coming back when my friend does."

"Maybe we'll work it out with him then. He'll probably be more reasonable than you're being right now, Vicky; pointing a gun at me and all."

"Don't kid yourself, Brett! The guy's a former Special Forces soldier. As a matter of fact, he also happens to be Megan's dad, and he's already pretty pissed off that she's not here! He'll definitely point a gun at you if you're still here, but the difference in him and I is that he'll pull the trigger before you have a chance to open your mouth."

"Megan's dad? Are you serious? Well, he's a little late if you ask me. I think Gareth was probably right; Megan and Aaron are dead by now. They either starved or somebody killed Aaron and took Megan! I think someone must have gotten Colleen like that, because she wouldn't have just left."

"That won't stop Eric Branson from searching all the way to Aaron's tribal lands. If she *is* alive, he'll find her. But I'm telling you, and you'd better pass it on to Gareth and Jeremy: Don't be here when he gets back, and don't bother trying to find me, because you won't! Good-bye Brett!"

Vicky turned and walked quickly towards the

hitching post where the horses were still tied. She looked over her shoulder and saw that Brett was still on his knees, watching her go. He didn't have it in him to try anything alone, and Vicky knew she was lucky it had been him they'd left to guard the horses. She doubted either Gareth or Jeremy would be so compliant.

As she approached the tethered animals, all three of them seemed to recognize her. Tucker, in particular, was excited to see her. She whispered his name and talked to all of them in a soothing voice, telling them she was happy they were back as she untied the reins. But another glance in Brett's direction revealed that he was up and running into the barn now that she was much farther away. She hoped like hell there wasn't another gun in there, and she didn't waste any time waiting to find out. Vicky grabbed Tucker's mane and pulled herself onto his bare back. She regretted for a moment that she didn't make an effort to get one of the saddles while she had Brett on the ground. It had crossed her mind, but it seemed too risky and would take too much time. She could get them later after Eric returned. She intended to take it slow anyway, so she didn't see why she couldn't ride Tucker bareback, no farther than she planned to go. She wheeled him around and nudged him with her heels and leading the other two with their reins in one hand, headed out through the ponderosas to the west at a trot. Now that she was riding, she knew where she wanted to go, but first, she needed to make a big circle around the open pasture, keeping far enough within the trees to stay out of sight in case Gareth and Jeremy returned early. Vicky smiled as she thought of the look that would be on Gareth's face when he came back and found out what happened. A part of her wished she could be there to see it, but the wiser part knew she needed to be long gone before then.

She was still within sight of the barn when the first gunshot rang out. A glance in that direction revealed Brett standing at the doorway aiming a handgun at her. The second shot hit one of the other two horses, and all hell broke loose when it jumped and tore away from her, causing all three animals to take off at a dead run. Vicky dropped the reins of the other one too and clung to Tucker's mane for her life, keeping her head low as he galloped away through the trees. Brett fired several more shots, but Vicky wasn't counting. She didn't know what kind of gun he had or how many rounds it had, but it could have been her grandpa's .44 Magnum, another of his guns they'd stolen. She'd made a huge mistake in hoping Brett didn't have another weapon, and she knew now she could have paid for it with her life. It was awful that one of the other horses had been hit, and she had no idea how bad it was because both of them had bolted in another direction and there was no telling how far they would run. She couldn't risk going back to look for them not knowing how much ammo Brett had or whether or not he would try to follow her. The one thing she did know was that he'd fired at her from way out of normal handgun range and he probably didn't care if he hit the horses or not. If she gave him another chance, he might get lucky next time despite the odds. By the time she managed to bring Tucker under control again, slowing him to a walk before she fell off, she'd created more than enough distance to be safe for the moment, as she was well out of sight of the barn and pasture. There was nothing to do now but press on and find a place to hole up, so she urged Tucker ahead while trying to bring her heart rate and breathing back under control. Shooting Brett while she had the chance would have been the smart thing to do, but she'd never even pointed a gun at another person before today. Vicky couldn't have killed him in cold blood, not then anyway. But after what had just happened, she made up her mind she would do what was necessary next time.

The destination she had in mind was a steep, rocky canyon only a couple of miles to the south. It was far enough away that Gareth and his friends wouldn't likely look there that afternoon, even if they began a diligent search for her. Vicky knew that it would take her another hour to reach it, considering the roundabout way that she had to go to get there, but it was the best option she knew of in the area for both a hideout and shelter. There were piles of truck-sized boulders in the bottom of the canyon, and a small stream that ran among them. The cave-like spaces between and underneath some of them would give her some options for getting out of the wind and building a small fire that couldn't be seen from afar. She reached down and felt the reassuring shape of the butane lighter in the front pocket of her jeans. It was the last one she had, but it was nearly full of fluid and she'd gotten pretty good at preparing her fire materials so that she needed only a couple of seconds to get the flames going. Out here tonight with nothing but the clothes she was wearing, a fire would be crucial.

Vicky found her way to the lower reaches of the creek after taking a circuitous route around the ranch pastures. She still proceeded slowly, knowing Gareth and Jeremy were out there somewhere, but she assumed they weren't anywhere nearby when she finally reached the mouth of the rocky canyon and turned into it. But she had barely gone a quarter mile in before a rifle shot rang out from somewhere quite close on the timbered ridge above. Convinced that she was the target, Vicky urged Tucker onward as fast as he could go up the rocky creek bed, just as a big mule deer buck coming from the other way splashed across the stream directly in front of her. There was a second rifle shot, and she heard a bullet ricochet off the rocks behind the running animal. Then she heard a shouted curse from the same direction as the gunshot when the buck disappeared into the brush. Vicky realized then that the shooter had been aiming at the deer and that she and Tucker must have startled it and frightened it away, causing the shot to miss. The shooter had to be Gareth or Jeremy, and she wondered if they had spotted her too. When she heard him yell again, she got her answer:

"HEY! STOP! THAT'S MY HORSE!"

It was Gareth! Vicky recognized his voice now without a doubt. She couldn't pinpoint exactly where he was, but apparently, he could see her, and she knew she needed to get out of the open fast. Vicky turned Tucker into the brush the way the deer had gone, frantic to duck out of Gareth's view before he could get his sights on her. She was glad she did when she heard him fire again. She doubted he could see her under the canopy of the trees, but she wasn't taking any chances. She urged Tucker on, deeper into the cover and up the slope away from the creek, knowing that staying out of sight and creating distance was the only thing keeping her alive.

FOUR

GARETH MABRY WAS HAVING A BAD DAY, BUT THAT was nothing new. He'd had a whole string of bad days in a row, but he'd really been looking forward to a break from it when he and Jeremy and Brett finally made their way back to the Singleton ranch. He knew full well that the old man would be pissed that they'd taken some of his horses, guns, and other stuff they needed, but he was going to make it up to him. He would explain why they did it—to try and save Megan from her own stupidity—and then he would apologize and admit that it was a mistake. Gareth had since come to realize that laying low in a place like that isolated ranch wasn't such a bad idea after all. It had seemed like a waste of time before, but he now realized that the situation everywhere had gotten so out of control that it was best just to focus on survival for now, especially since he didn't know where to find another resistance group to join. The ranch offered a better possibility of avoiding trouble than any place else he'd been since leaving Boulder, so after what happened to Colleen, Gareth decided to cut his losses and come back. Further searching for Megan seemed futile, and while he'd really been into her at first, and thought she saw things his way, as time went by that proved not to be the case. She wasn't interested in helping bring about change, and like her roommate, Vicky, all she was thinking about was finding a place to hide out and running home to family. The idea of it made Gareth sick at first but seeing how everybody else at the resistance campsite had scattered too, he went along with them at the time. There would have been enough of them to hold out and fight if everyone was committed, but sadly, that wasn't the case.

Gareth had learned a lot from the Indian dude, Aaron, but like Megan and Vicky, Aaron wanted to avoid confrontation. He left the campus because he knew staying there wouldn't end well, and he'd only come to the resistance camp in the first place because the girls invited him. Gareth had only met him once or twice before that, and he soon found out that Aaron wasn't down for helping the struggle either, even though he was descended from tough people with a history of standing up to the same government. Gareth thought that Aaron would be eager to help bring it down now, but it turned out he was weak and wasn't a fighter. He wanted to get back to the traditional lands of his people where he had relatives, so he could hide out and pretend none of this was happening. He claimed to be like his ancestors, but he wasn't a warrior. The only thing he had in common with the Apaches of old was his love of the outdoors. Gareth saw early on after the resistance camp was routed that Aaron was very comfortable with backcountry travel and living off the land, much more so than anyone else in their small group, and without his help, they probably wouldn't have made it there at all. While they still went hungry much of the time along the way, what little they did have to eat was the direct result of Aaron's hunting skills. Gareth learned what he could from him, but the two of them were still at odds from the beginning. It was obvious that Aaron was becoming infatuated with Megan, and the more time they spent together, the more she seemed to enjoy his attention. If she'd simply broken up with him for some other reason, Gareth wouldn't have been so bothered by it. But as it was, he felt Aaron had deliberately stolen her away by making her promises that he couldn't keep. Vicky seemed content enough to stay at the ranch with her grandparents, as she was close to them anyway and knew getting to Portland wasn't happening. Megan, however, was restless there, and felt compelled to try and make it home to Florida no matter how difficult it might be to get there. Heading south to the lands of Aaron's people in New Mexico was a step in the right direction in her mind, and so she'd simply left with him, no doubt believing whatever BS he told her about helping her get home from there.

Gareth was sick of hanging around the ranch

anyway, as were Brett and Jeremy, and Jeremy's girl-friend, Colleen. Going after Megan and Aaron would give them a change of scenery, but more than anything, Gareth wanted to make him pay and make her realize what a loser Aaron was. The old man had given Megan and Aaron horses, but he had plenty more, so he wouldn't miss the ones Gareth and his friends needed, so they left before dawn a couple days later, leaving Vicky behind there with her grandma and grandpa. He had no reason to doubt that the three of them would still be there when he returned today with Jeremy and Brett. The ranch was sufficiently remote that only a couple of the old man's friends had stopped by during all the weeks they'd all been there together, so Gareth had no reason to expect what they found today when they rode in. It came as a total shock, both to him and to his companions.

It wasn't like he had a lot of sympathy for the old man and his wife though. In his conversations with them while he'd been here before, Gareth gleaned that they were supporters of all the things the resistance was fighting to bring down. He didn't bother to argue or tell them anything of his own opinions because he knew it wouldn't do any good. Vicky had already warned them to keep quiet about any involvement with that before they got there, but Gareth figured she probably ran her mouth afterward and really made him out to be a total bad guy when he and his friends took the horses and guns. He'd expected to have some explaining to do when he came back if he hoped to get any more supplies from the ranch or stay there again, but he hadn't expected to find two graves and a burned down house. But as soon as he read the marker between the graves, he felt sure that Vicky must have somehow survived, he just wasn't sure she was still around. Finding military rations in the barn didn't lead him to believe she was the one using them, because it was the first time he'd seen anything like that around there. Vicky's grandparents instead had more traditional stockpiles of canned goods and other non-perishable foods; enough, in fact, that if this hadn't happened, the supplies on hand would have nearly been enough to see all of them through the winter, especially if they could supplement it with an occasional deer or elk kill. Gareth didn't quite know what to make of finding those MREs in the barn, but Jeremy suggested they might have been left there by soldiers that attacked the place and killed the Singletons. Gareth thought the only reason they would do something like that though was if they somehow found out the old rancher was harboring members of the resistance.

"With the way Megan and Vicky were running their mouths to all their friends about coming here, that's got to be it. The goons got word that a bunch of college kids were heading up here to hole up, so they sent their thugs up here to wipe it off the map. Probably figured the old man was complicit with the cause."

"That sounds about right," Jeremy had agreed. "It might explain why Vicky's missing too. If they didn't kill her outright, they probably took her in for interrogation if they suspected her of terrorism."

"Yeah, but who would have dug those graves?" Brett had wondered.

None of them had a good answer for that, but they had come all the way back here and they had nowhere else to go, so Gareth thought they ought to at least hang around until they could come up with a new plan. After moving their stuff into the barn and resting a while, he was ready to go out and have a look around the property and see if he could find more clues as to what may have happened there. Jeremy went with him, and like always these days, they had their weapons in hand, both for defense against whoever they might encounter and for taking a shot at any game animal that might present itself.

They had wandered quite far afield and were up on the ridge above the opening of the large canyon south of the ranch pasturelands when he spotted the big mule deer buck some 300 yards below, walking towards the little creek winding through the bottom. It was a long shot, but Gareth wasn't going to pass up the chance at getting that much meat. He whispered to Jeremy to wait while he slipped down a little closer to try and close the gap. But the buck had not quite reached the stream when something startled it and it suddenly bolted across. Gareth squeezed off a round from the .308 and saw his bullet kick up dust where it hit the rocks; a clean miss. He levered another round into the Winchester and fired a second shot, only to miss again. When he yelled out in fury at his bad luck another movement just downstream caught his eye. *There was someone on horseback down there, probably only a hundred feet from where the buck had been standing when he missed his shot!* The rider had spurred the horse into a run, heading into cover behind the fleeing deer. Gareth swept the riflescope across the horse and rider before they disappeared and confirmed without a doubt what he already thought he saw: *It was Tucker! The same Appaloosa he'd rode in on that very morning!* He tried to focus on the rider before he lost sight of them. He was sure it wasn't Brett though, because whoever it was, they were much smaller, and riding bareback, something Brett, who could barely ride at all, would never attempt.

His first impression was confirmed when the rider turned and looked back just before the horse entered the woods.

Gareth was almost certain it was a girl or woman, and he yelled for her to stop, but his shouts went unheeded. He fired a wild shot into the trees to vent his frustration, but the horse and rider were already gone.

"What in the hell?" Jeremy asked, as he came rushing down to where Gareth was to see what was going on.

"Someone's stolen my horse! I think it was Vicky, but I couldn't tell for sure!"

"But how would she? Brett was watching the horses!"

"I don't know, but I'm going after her. Go back and get Brett and the other two horses if they're still there! She can't get out of this canyon on that horse. It's way too steep farther up. If I follow her right now, she won't be able to circle back around the way she came in, but I'll need you and Brett to help me keep her boxed in until we catch her. So hurry!"

"Got it! I just hope Brett's still there when I get there. I don't know how she could have gotten Tucker right out from under his nose like that!"

"Because Brett's an idiot! He was probably asleep or else had his mind on Colleen like always and wasn't paying attention. We'll find out what happened later. Just go!"

Jeremy worked his way back down the steep, wooded ridge and then took off at a run as soon as he reached the open pasturelands. The whole time he ran he wondered how Brett could have been so careless that Vicky could steal one of those horses with him so close by. He hoped Gareth was right when he said there wasn't another way out of that canyon, because if there was, he would never catch up to her on foot. He wondered now if she'd been there all along, watching them since they arrived, and he figured that yes, that had to be it. She'd waited until he and Gareth left and then taken Tucker when Brett wasn't looking. This really sucked, because if Gareth didn't get that horse back, one of them was going to be without a ride. Jeremy didn't even consider the possibility that all of them might be, at least not until he finally caught sight of the barn and house site and saw there were no horses tied to the hitching post at all.

Jeremy stopped running and made a cautious approach to the barn, wondering now if something may have happened to Brett too. When he got to the gate, he saw that the saddles were still inside, but there was no sign of Brett. He continued on out to the hitching post and then down the drive towards the road. It was there that he spotted Brett making his way through the woods just west of the drive. When Brett saw him, he quickly ran back to meet him. Brett was out of breath, frustrated and angry.

"I've been trying to catch the other two horses! That bitch, *Vicky,* took Tucker! I tried to stop her, but I missed."

"I know. Gareth saw her! He's going after her now. She's in that canyon a couple of miles to the south. Gareth said there's no other way out, but we need to get back there in case she tries to slip around him. Do you know where the other two horses are?"

"Yeah, I've been trying to catch them! I was close, but right before you got here, they just ran up the road a short distance and went back into the woods. I think I might have accidentally hit one of them when I was shooting at her, but it must not have been all that bad, because they were both still running. Vicky had all three of them when she left. She was leading the other two, but she let go of them when I shot at her. Come on! Let's go down to the road and see if we can spot them. We may be able to split up or something and round them up."

Jeremy followed him as he led the way to where he'd last seen the horses. As they walked, Brett told him what had happened, and how Vicky had walked up to him like everything was cool, and then suddenly pointed a pistol at him and took his rifle. He also told him that she said she wasn't alone here.

"Megan's dad?" Jeremy said in disbelief, when Brett told him Vicky claimed he was nearby, and on his way back. "That sounds pretty unlikely to me, dude. I'll bet she was just making that shit up to bluff you. She's by herself, or she wouldn't still be out here!"

"I don't know man. I don't know where she'd come up with something like that if it was bullshit. And what about those Army rations we found? You know that was military stuff. Gareth said so too. It makes sense that it could be him. You know Megan said her dad was some kind of Special Forces dude. Vicky said so too. She said he was a real badass, and that we'd better not be around here when he shows up.

"Well, I don't see him. Do you? Gareth didn't see him when he spotted her heading up that canyon either, so I don't think we need to worry about him right now. We just need to catch those horses and get back there to help Gareth find her before dark. It's gonna suck to only have two horses if she gets away with Tucker. Or maybe only one if the one you shot dies."

"He's not gonna die. I thought she was too far away to actually hit when I shot anyway. I was just hoping I would get lucky, but I sure didn't mean to hit one of the horses. I can't even tell you how pissed off I was after she had me at gunpoint like that, making me crawl on my knees like a dog or something."

"Yeah, it's too bad I wasn't here to get a video of that! That would be funny as hell to post if there was a way to even get online anymore!"

"Yeah, whatever! It wouldn't be funny if it happened to you. I guess I was stupid to trust her, but she did come walking up being all friendly and all, like nothing ever happened."

"It's stupid to trust *anybody* these days, Brett. Gareth keeps saying that over and over. He *is* right, you know!"

Brett didn't answer, and Jeremy knew that he was probably feeling pretty stupid indeed right about now. Not only did he lose the horses because of trusting Vicky; he also lost the .22 Magnum rifle that he'd been carrying. That was a shame, because it had proven useful for hunting smaller game and the ammo for it, which they had plenty of, was much lighter than the ammo for the other rifles and the shotgun they still had.

Jeremy was in fact, carrying the shotgun now, as Gareth had suggested when they went out hunting in case, they jumped a deer and got an opportunity for a running shot at close range. Loaded with double-aught buckshot, the 12-gauge made it easier to hit moving targets, and it was good in thick brush at close range, something that crossed Jeremy's mind now as they entered the woods where Brett had last seen the horses. Although he wanted to dismiss it as something Vicky probably made up to frighten Brett, what if Megan's father really *was* around?

Someone had to bring those MREs out there to the barn, and the dude *was* supposed to be some kind of military guy. If he did leave them there, then maybe it wasn't soldiers who killed the old couple and burned down the house. He asked Brett if Vicky had mentioned it, but Brett said their conversation was much too short to get into that. Whoever had done it hadn't left much of anything but the barn. All of the remaining horses were gone, as were the vehicles and most of the useful tools around the place. How Vicky managed to escape he didn't know, but after what she'd pulled today, Jeremy figured she was probably more cunning than he'd thought. And needless to say, he was a little on edge as they spread out through the trees looking for the two horses. Jeremy took the lead since he was the one with the shotgun, and because he was so nervous, he had a round in the chamber and his finger already lightly resting on the trigger as he quietly pushed his way through a thicket.

A sound unmistakably made by an animal in pain caused him to glance over his shoulder at Brett to confirm he'd heard it too. When Brett nodded, Jeremy turned and pushed on towards the noise. *It had to be the wounded horse!* When he reached the edge of the brush, he saw that he was right. The palest of the three Appaloosas was down on the ground on its side, and a man dressed like a cowboy was crouching over it, doing something to it. Jeremy's exit from the bushes wasn't as stealthy as he'd planned and when he snapped a dry branch, the stranger, whose back had been to him at first, quickly rose to a standing position and spun around, pointing a short rifle in the direction of the unexpected sound.

Seeing the weapon in the man's hand, Jeremy reacted without thinking. He pulled the trigger of the shotgun, sending the load of buckshot at the man from a distance of less than 25 yards. As the stranger dropped to his knees, his rifle and cowboy hat falling to the ground as he bent over, clutching his abdomen, Jeremy was surprised to see that he was much older than he'd expected. The man's longish hair and beard were completely silver. There was confusion in his eyes as he tried to focus them on Jeremy, who was standing there not knowing what to do next when Brett stepped out of the brush beside him. His hands were shaking as he clung to the shotgun, already regretting what he'd done as he watched the growing stain of dark blood that was seeping through the man's shirt just above the beltline. Jeremy glanced at Brett, who was just standing there open-mouthed as he took in the scene.

"He had a gun!" Jeremy said. "I thought he was gonna shoot me first! I had to do it!"

"What was he doing to the horse? Did you see the other one?"

Jeremy said he didn't know, but then it occurred to him that maybe the old man wasn't alone. He mentioned this to Brett, telling him to keep the revolver ready, just in case. Then the two of them moved closer to the wounded man, who made no attempt to reach for the fallen lever-action rifle he'd been carrying. A low whinny from farther back in the trees startled Jeremy again, and that's when he saw that there were two more horses tethered there, one saddled and the other heavily laden with packs. Neither of them was the other Appaloosa they were looking for, though. The old man was still clutching his belly and coughing and sputtering as he tried to say something. Jeremy turned his attention back to him, feeling sick when he saw how much blood now soaked the man's clothes and the ground around him. Brett was as pale as a ghost too. Neither of them had ever shot anyone before today.

"I wasn't gonna shoot," the old man finally mumbled. "Just trying to see to that horse, until you surprised me. Are you the one that shot him too?"

Jeremy glanced at the bullet wound in the horse's left flank. It looked a lot worse than what Brett had described. The animal had lost a lot of blood and had finally fallen, unable to get back up. Jeremy didn't know how the old man came to find him, but he could see that he'd been using a rag to try and stop the animal's bleeding. And now he was going to bleed out himself if he didn't get help.

"Look man, I'm sorry. I thought you were about to shoot, and I just reacted. How bad is it? We will help you."

"Bad enough I ain't gonna make it, son. If that horse is yours, you'd best put him out of his misery and don't worry about me."

It had taken all the strength he had for the man to utter those words. Now he slumped from his knees and fell over onto his side to the ground. Jeremy could see more blood from the exit wounds where the buckshot had torn through his back.

"We've got to help him, Brett! Maybe if we put pressure on these wounds, we can stop the bleeding!"

"With what?"

"Anything! That rag, whatever you can find. Just grab something!"

Jeremy's hands were soon sticky with blood as he knelt over the old man's body, trying desperately to stop the steady flow of blood pumping between his fingers. It seemed hopeless, even when Brett joined him. The old man seemed oblivious to their efforts now anyway, and Jeremy was pretty sure that he was about to lose consciousness. Brett was talking to him now, telling him to hang in there, and that it was going to be all right, but Jeremy knew it wasn't. He had shot a man in cold blood, and there was no way to undo it now. Jeremy looked up at Brett again and was surprised to see a sudden look of terror written on his face. It had nothing to do with the horror of watching a man die though, because this time Brett was looking over Jeremy's shoulder towards the trees behind him. Jeremy turned around to see why and found himself staring into the muzzle of an assault rifle pointed directly at his face by a dark-bearded and very serious-looking man dressed in green camo clothing. Then, he heard a woman scream "BOB!" just before the bearded guy's boot slammed into his chest, sending him cartwheeling into Brett and causing both of them to sprawl onto the ground in a heap. The shotgun was completely out of reach now and Brett's revolver had gone flying too. It wouldn't have mattered anyway. Before he could process what was happening, a woman had appeared on the scene too and was standing over him with a similar rifle of her own pointed at his face. Out of the corner of his eye, Jeremy could see that the bearded man was now crouching over the body of the man he'd shot. He saw him turn and looked back at his female companion, shaking his head. "He's gone, Shauna!"

"DON'T SHOOT!" Jeremy pleaded. "It was an accident! I swear it was!"

FIVE

ERIC BRANSON WAS NO HORSE WRANGLER AND certainly not a horse whisperer. He was doing well enough just to ride at all. It had been years since he'd climbed into a saddle, and the times before that few and far between. Trail riding at a walking pace was one thing but galloping through heavy timber wasn't something he was interested in, so he let Shauna do that. She was much better at this equestrian stuff by far, and he watched with interest as she spurred her own mount to run down the second of the two horses they'd spotted out by the road. Whatever she said to it as she nudged her own horse to its side seemed to work, and the frightened animal appeared to calm down and trust her. In a moment she had taken control of its reins and was leading it back to where Eric waited astride his own mount.

"Is that one injured too?" he asked, as she drew near enough to speak to her in a low voice.

"Not that I can tell. He's just scared I think, and it's understandable, considering that the other one was shot."

Eric nodded. Coming upon the two horses this close to the ranch had been a surprise. One of them had a bullet wound in its hindquarters and had been limping along near the ditch at the edge of the road trying to keep up with its companion when the three of them rode up. Bob immediately spotted the wound and said the injured horse looked like it was hit pretty bad. When both of the frightened animals took off at the sight of them, the wounded one made it only a few hundred feet off the road before collapsing and going down. The other one continued running until Shauna caught up and managed to coax it to a stop.

If the horses hadn't been wearing bridles and bits, Eric would have thought little of it, but that was clear evidence *someone* had been riding them, and they'd arrived here recently too. Other than Vicky, there wasn't supposed to be anyone around the property, and there hadn't been when he'd left her in the barn earlier that very morning. Eric had cautioned both Bob and Shauna to keep quiet and keep their eyes open as they spotted them. Once they secured the second horse, Eric planned to circle around through the woods and approach the barn and burned-out house site to investigate while Bob was checking to see if he could do anything for the wounded one.

Though he'd only known him for a few hours, Eric could tell that Bob Barham probably knew more about horses than anyone he knew, and horses were exactly what Eric had been looking for when he'd unexpectedly met the man on the trail. Even more unexpected though, was that his ex-wife, Shauna, was riding with the old man and that they were on their way to the same ranch he'd just left. Eric had known Shauna planned to go there, of course, because it was her note that pointed him to it in the first place, but he'd expected to find her and Jonathan already there, hopefully with their daughter, Megan. Instead, he'd found a burned-down home, two graves and the frightened girl that had been Megan's roommate before their college life was ripped apart. But finding Vicky meant at least Eric had an idea where Megan went, and now, thanks to running into Shauna and Bob Barham on the trail, he had the means to follow. All they had to do was get back to the barn and get Vicky, and then return to Bob's cabin where Jonathan was laid up with a broken leg. There they would make their preparations. Riding all the way to northern New Mexico through the backcountry of the divide was going to be an expedition, but that was the route Megan had taken and nothing would stop Eric from tracking her down. According to Vicky, she'd left with just one companion, another college kid about her age named Aaron. Vicky said Aaron knew his way around in the outdoors, but still, it was just the two of them on their own, facing unknown threats, and Eric and Shauna had already seen enough on the way here to know what that could mean.

Shauna was understandably crushed when Eric told her she wasn't going to have her anticipated reunion with Megan at Vicky's grandparents' ranch.

"But at least we know where she's headed and with who," Eric said. "We just need to get there as soon as we can and hope they made it. At least we know now that she made it this far, and that she was fine when she left. They left with horses, supplies and weapons for defense and hunting. If everything Vicky told me about Aaron is true, I'd say their odds of finding their way through the mountains were good."

"It's not just finding their way and having enough to eat though," Shauna had said. "I learned that with what happened to Jonathan. One minute he was fine, looking for a path, and the next he was down with a broken leg, all because of a single misstep. He would have died then and there if he'd been alone, or if we hadn't been so lucky that it happened close to Bob's cabin."

Eric couldn't argue with that. After hearing the story, he knew Jonathan owed his life to Bob. It was fortunate that they had stumbled upon one of the good guys who was willing to help. And now Bob wanted to continue helping them. In fact, he'd insisted:

"If you're planning to ride all the way to New Mexico, you're going to need me along, I'll tell you that. Your lady here has told me about your background and I respect your military training and combat experience, but if you've never done it, wrangling horses through these mountains ain't as easy as it looks, especially this time of year with the weather that's coming. Besides that, these animals are worth more to me than anything you could offer to pay me for them. So, it's a package deal or nothing. I'm not doing it for what I can get out of it though, or because I've heard your wife's story and know how much you two want to find your daughter. The fact is, I was already getting a bad case of cabin fever before she and Jonathan showed up. I know it's safer to stay put with everything that's going on and all, but I've always wanted to make a trip like that and now I've got a good excuse. I'm an old man anyway, and I ain't gonna live forever whether I hide out in my cabin or not. So, I may as well see some of the country while I still can."

Eric understood the man's reluctance to part with his horses, but he hadn't expected him to volunteer for hardships such as they would face with nothing in it for him but the adventure. It was immediately obvious upon meeting him though that Bob not only knew how to handle horses, but he was completely at home in the outdoors. That didn't tell Eric anything about how he would handle himself in a hostile encounter when the bullets started flying, but no one knew that until they were there. He and Shauna had already survived many firefights and there would likely be more to come along the way. He didn't really like the idea of bringing aboard a total stranger, but then, he'd done the same with Jonathan and that had worked out far better than

SCOTT B. WILLIAMS

expected. He went along with the idea for the moment, knowing he could make a final decision later after they got Vicky and returned to Bob's cabin for Jonathan. He could see that the poor girl was terrified when he left and afraid that he wouldn't return at all, and he could understand why. She'd been traumatized by what had happened to her grandparents, not to mention all she'd been through since she'd left the university with Megan. Eric had learned some of the details from her already, but he was sure too that she'd left out a lot that she could tell him later about both their ordeal and Megan. Seeing Shauna would likely help put her mind at ease, and there would be plenty of time to talk once they made it to Bob's and began their preparations. Taking her on as another responsibility to look out for wasn't ideal, but Eric couldn't just leave her on her own. She was a close friend of Megan's, and unless she wanted to stay at Bob's cabin, or go elsewhere, the decision was made for him. They would take her south with them, whatever risk it might entail.

"Well, all of you are welcome to stay as long as you like," Bob said, when Eric mentioned it "but if you're planning on riding through these mountains before all the passes are snowed in, you don't need to wait too long. If you do, you'll be in for a spell of cabin fever up at my place!"

"We won't waste any time getting going," Eric said. "I hope Jonathan will be healed up enough to ride."

"Yeah, it won't be comfortable, but I'm sure he can

66

do it. He's young and tough and can deal with the pain. It'll be a while though before that break heals up enough for him to do much walking, so riding is his only choice unless he wants to stay behind."

"He won't. Even though Shauna says your place is really something, Jonathan will want to go with us and I'm sure he'll deal with the pain. He'll ride one of those horses if it kills him. That kid's as stubborn as my ex-wife! If nearly getting her hand shot off didn't stop her, a broken leg won't stop Jonathan!"

Bob grinned when Shauna gave Eric a hard look. "I'd say you're all stubborn if anybody asked, and that's a good thing these days! You'd have to be to make a trip like you did, all the way from the bottom of Florida."

Eric couldn't argue with that. He'd reflected on his journey as they fell into single file and turned back south on the Continental Divide Trail. The path was too narrow in most places to ride two abreast on the horses, so Eric brought up the rear behind Shauna, while Bob Barham led the way with his single packhorse in tow. As he rode, adjusting to the unfamiliar feel of the saddle, Eric reflected on the setbacks and obstacles that had come between him and his ever-elusive objective of finding his daughter and getting her to safety. Scanning the snowy peaks that filled the horizon to either side of the trail, Eric knew he had indeed come a long way from 'the bottom of Florida.' He thought back to that dark, rainy morning when he'd made landfall at Jupiter Inlet, hopeful that he would quickly reach his objective just a few miles away. If Megan and Shauna had still been at home, he would have too. He had planned his insertion the way he usually did when working such a mission, landing reasonably close to the target, but far enough away to give him several options if needed. He'd come prepared for anything he might run into in a hostile environment, and that had certainly felt strange, considering that it was his home country and state into which he was slipping ashore in a kayak full of weapons and ammo. It had been immediately obvious though, even in the dark, that everything on that familiar coast had changed since he'd last seen it. The reality he found at home far exceeded the rumors he'd heard while still abroad, and he was to soon find out that the dangers here in America would put to the test *all* of his skills and experience. And the more he'd seen since that first night, the more Eric wondered if life in his home country would ever be the same.

He'd succeeded in finding Shauna and getting her and his dad out of Florida, and now Bart was in a place of relative safety with his brother, Keith. Now he'd found Shauna again after being separated from her and Jonathan because of a delay in the mission he'd agreed to do for Lieutenant Holton back east. Eric still had a lot he wanted to talk to Shauna about, filling in and getting details about their separate journeys, but there hadn't been time for that yet. They had ridden in silence for the most part while on the narrow trail, and more so as they neared the ranch on the gravel road. But now they'd been interrupted by the discovery of the two horses. The only question was who were their riders, and where were they now?

"Why don't you take that one and my horse too and go check on Bob and the injured one," Eric said, as he swung down out of the saddle. "I'm going to make a sweep around the back side of this pine grove and see if I see anything. If I don't make contact, I'll circle back to where you are and let you know. Then I'll slip down to the barn and make sure Vicky's okay," he said, as he checked his M4 and handed her the reins to the mare he'd been riding.

"I could go..." Shauna's sentence was cut short by the sudden blast of a gunshot in Bob's direction. Bob was only about 200 yards away, but completely out of sight in the woods.

"That was a shotgun!" Eric whispered, "It wasn't Bob! Let's tie off the horses so they won't follow and go! Stick close behind me and move as quietly as you can!" They did, and Eric started in the direction of the sound, expecting that he might hear more shots or return fire from Bob's rifle or pistol, but the woods fell silent. It wasn't until he had closed the gap, stalking carefully and using all available cover to keep out of sight, that he heard something else—*voices!*

They were male voices, two at least, and neither sounded like Bob Barham. They seemed quite agitated from their tones, but he couldn't make out what they were saying until he moved closer and heard one of them saying he didn't mean to do it, but he'd been scared. Eric knew then it was Bob Barham that had been shot, even before he crept close enough to get his rifle sights on the two young men who were bent over him, where he lay curled up on the ground, unmoving. Eric's finger was on the trigger of his M4 and he could have easily taken both of the men down before they knew he was there, but he could see that they'd put down their weapons and were frantically trying to do something for Bob as they talked about how to stop the bleeding. Eric glanced back at Shauna before moving in, trusting she would cover him if he needed her.

When he broke out of the concealment of the bushes, he saw at a glance the amount of blood surrounding the fallen man and on the hands of the two young strangers who were trying to stop it. They were completely caught off guard by his sudden appearance and Eric took advantage of that fact by planting a front kick in the chest of the nearest one that launched him into his companion and put them both on the ground. When he saw that Shauna was at his side with her rifle to keep them there, he grabbed the shotgun he saw and tossed it into the bushes. Then Eric dropped to a knee at Bob's side to check his status. It only took a moment to see that he didn't have a chance. The old man had taken a load of buckshot square in the midsection. His eyes were already fixed with an empty stare as Eric checked for a pulse. Bob Barham didn't make it.

When Eric turned back to Shauna to tell her, she

was standing over the two strangers, covering them while the one he'd kicked began pleading for his life, saying that it was an accident, and that he didn't mean to kill anyone. Eric would have shot them both on the spot if either made the slightest move to reach for a weapon or run, but he wanted to know who they were first, and why they were here, on ranch land belonging to Vicky's grandparents. Seeing that there were two of them, it was reasonable to conclude they were the missing riders he'd wondered about when they found the two horses.

"I thought he was going to shoot me! Honest, I swear! He had a rifle when he turned around! I didn't think I had a choice!" The terrified young man explained.

"Who are you? And what are you doing here? Is that your horse?" Eric nodded at the horse Bob had been attending.

"Yes! I... I mean, no... not really! Actually, it belonged to Vicky's grandpa, but he let us use some of his horses. We were here because we were just bringing them back!"

"Vicky's grandpa? You know Vicky? How do you know her, and who are you?"

"Yes, we know her. We're her friends! I'm Jeremy, and this is my buddy, Brett."

Eric glared at both of them. He knew they were names Vicky had mentioned. Jeremy was the only one talking, so Eric focused on him. The other kid, Brett, seemed too shaken to utter a word.

"Vicky told me the horses were stolen. She told me

some of the friends she brought here took them, and she mentioned both of you by name! She said you all left to try and catch up to Megan Branson." Eric grabbed the boy by the collar and dragged him to his feet, pulling his face up close to his as he stared into his eyes with an intensity that made it clear he'd kill. "Do you know where Megan is?" He gave him a hard shake. "HAVE YOU SEEN HER?"

"NO! I haven't seen her since she left! Gareth wanted to find her and talk to her, because she was his girlfriend, and he wanted her to come back. But we never found her! We tried but we couldn't catch up to them. And then we ran into trouble and lost all our supplies. We came back here because we had no place else to go!"

"Gareth!" Eric said in disgust, pushing Jeremy back with enough force that he landed hard on his backside again next to Brett, who was now staring at him intently, as if he'd finally figured something out.

"You're Megan's dad, aren't you?" He asked. "Vicky wasn't lying!"

Eric's gaze turned to Brett, who began backing up on the ground and looking like he wished he'd never opened his mouth. It did him little good though, because Eric leapt on top of him, slamming him flat and bending low over his face so that his every word would be understood. "When did you talk to Vicky, boy? And where is she now?" Brett's eyes were wide, and he was shaking so uncontrollably that he could barely speak. Eric filled in the blanks for him. "I *am* Megan's dad, that's right! And

72

when I left here this morning, her friend, Vicky was in the barn down there next to what's left of the house. I'm back here to get her, and you'd better tell me that she's still there waiting for me and that she's all right!"

"She took the horses!" Jeremy said. "We didn't know she was here when we came back. I went hunting with Gareth and while we were gone, Vicky came sneaking up and pulled a gun on Brett. She made him give her his rifle and then she rode off on Gareth's horse, leading the other two. That's one of them right there!" Jeremy pointed at the wounded horse next to Bob's body.

"So where is she now?" Eric let go of Brett and stood up, looking at both of them. "Why were those two horses running loose and how did that one get a bullet wound?"

"I don't know!" Brett said. "They were fine when she rode off with them. I guess they got away from her. I saw them out on the road and was trying to catch them when Jeremy came back here to get me. He said he and Gareth had seen somebody out there where they were hunting, riding Gareth's horse."

"It's true!" Jeremy said. "I didn't see them, but Gareth did. He didn't know for sure if it was Vicky though. He just knew somebody was on his horse and that it looked like a girl. He went after her on foot and he sent me back here to get Brett and the other two horses, and that's when I found out that it really *was* Vicky, and that she'd taken all three of the horses, but the other two were up here somewhere. We were just trying to round them up when we came upon your friend. He was bent down over that one that's on the ground, and when he heard me coming, he stood up with the gun and I thought he was gonna kill me. I figured it was him that shot that horse. It had to be, because there's nobody else around here."

"I can assure you that Bob Barham didn't shoot a horse!" Shauna screamed. "That man loved horses more than anyone I've ever met!"

"He didn't shoot the horse," Eric said. "It was already wounded when we first spotted it. We just came down from the pass, on the trail that begins where this road ends. Bob wanted to see if he could help it while she and I went to catch the other one."

"I'm so sorry about what happened," Jeremy said, a genuine look of remorse on his face. "I've never shot anybody in my life, but we've already had people trying to kill us since we came out here to the mountains. I was scared to death when I saw him with that gun."

"We'll deal with that later," Eric said. "What I want you to do right now is show me the place where you saw that rider on the other horse. I think you know now it was Vicky. You'd better hope she's okay and that your friend Gareth doesn't try to hurt her!"

"Gareth won't do anything to her," Brett said. "He just wants the horse. We'd be stuck out here without horses, now that we know Vicky's grandparents are dead and everything that was here has been either burned up or stolen. Besides, nobody's gonna mess with Vicky as long as she's got that pistol. I thought she was about to shoot me with it. I really did!"

"That's why I gave it to her," Eric said, "to shoot anybody that needed shooting until I got back here to do it myself!" Eric gave Brett a hard look that let him know he still hadn't ruled the two of them out of that category.

SIX

VICKY FELT HER HEART POUNDING AS SHE BENT LOW over Tucker's neck, dodging low-hanging spruce branches as she guided him up the steep slope on the west side of the drainage. She now knew for sure she was dealing with a group of desperate and deranged young men, if she didn't know it before. Brett hadn't hesitated to open fire on her to try and stop her from escaping with the horses, and after his third shot, long after the deer he'd been shooting at had vanished, she knew Gareth was quite willing to kill her too. Vicky began to second-guess her actions now: *Maybe she'd made a terrible mistake, taking those horses... Maybe she should have just found a place to survive the night and waited for Eric Branson to show up....* She'd known when she did it that it was a bold move, but in her mind, she was doing it for her late grandpa. The horses belonged to him and those three users who'd betrayed him didn't deserve to get away with them. They didn't care one bit about the animals anyway; that was obvious by the way both Brett and Gareth had fired indiscriminately in their direction. Vicky wondered how bad the other gelding Brett had hit was hurt. He'd been able to run off, but that didn't necessarily mean it wasn't a serious wound.

With the horses gone, her three pursuers were desperate now, and Vicky knew that meant they'd do anything. From the looks of them when she saw them riding in, they were quite desperate before too. They didn't come back here because they actually intended to return the horses to her grandpa, as Brett had said, but because they were hungry, and out of other options. Whatever or whoever they'd encountered out there in the mountains had convinced them to give up their pursuit of Megan and anything else they had in mind when they left here the first time. They'd come back without Colleen, and Vicky could only wonder what fate had befallen her because those three had failed to protect her. Whatever had happened though, they had managed to save themselves. She knew there was a lot Brett wasn't telling her, and that she'd probably never know the truth. Whether they were responsible for Colleen's disappearance or not, Vicky was under no delusion that they would do anything less than kill her if they could catch her now. Not only had they returned to find nothing here to sustain them, but she'd deprived them of their only means of transportation as well. She was fighting hard to overcome the fear that gripped her as she realized how serious her situation really was.

The weight of her grandpa's old varmint rifle across her back was comforting, but Vicky wished she had something better than a .22 Magnum. She didn't know a whole lot about firearms, but she knew enough to know that she was outmatched with just a low-capacity bolt-action in such a small caliber. Eric's Glock that was tucked in the back of her waistband again was far more suitable for defense against humans, but Vicky knew that like all handguns, it was designed for close range encounters. Neither it nor the Remington was a match for the high-powered deer rifle Gareth was shooting, especially since it was likely that it was her grandpa's favorite .308 that had an excellent scope mounted on it. That one was among the several they had stolen, and she'd watched both Gareth and Jeremy leaving the barn earlier with long guns in their hands. Regardless of what they were carrying, she knew she was both outgunned and outnumbered, even if Brett didn't manage to join them in their search.

Vicky couldn't afford to give them an opportunity to use those longer-range weapons against her, and the only way to avoid that was to stay out of sight. For now, the terrain and the heavy forest cover was working in her favor but taking advantage of that meant staying on the timbered slopes. Farther up the canyon, where it became steeper and rockier, she knew the trees thinned out. Even worse, the head of the drainage was effectively a box canyon, far too steep for riding. She knew the topography there well, as she'd been there many times with her grandpa, who took her to see the series of small waterfalls on the upper reaches of the creek. Vicky had loved the place at first sight as a little girl; especially the huge boulders that seemed to have been piled up around the creek by a giant. She'd loved exploring the grottos and caverns the spaces between them created, and it was among those boulders that she'd hoped to find shelter for the night when she first took off with the horses. That was out of the question now though, of course. Gareth knew she was here, and she was pretty sure he'd explored this canyon before too and would know that he had her in a trap.

She wouldn't have entered it at all if she'd thought Gareth and Jeremy might roam so far from the barn that afternoon. But it was too late now. She couldn't simply turn around and ride out, because from the vantage point from which he'd fired his rifle, Gareth could see the entirety of the lower end of the drainage, especially in the open area through which she would have to pass in order to exit. And for all she knew he might leave Jeremy there to watch that exit while he followed after her. She had no choice but to keep going up, even though she knew it led to a dead end, at least for Tucker. And while she was still mounted for now, riding gave her little advantage here, as speed was out of the question, the horse unable to safely walk any faster than a person could. In order to escape the canyon, Vicky would have to leave him behind. The only way out was to literally climb out with her hands and feet, pulling herself up a series of steep rock faces to reach the canyon rim.

The only way it *wouldn't* come to that was if she could stay ahead of her pursuers until dark. She was already in the deep shadows of the canyon walls and in another hour and a half, she knew it would be fully dark there. If she could stay hidden until then, Gareth and Jeremy might decide to hold off until daylight returned. They would be facing the same cold in the coming night as she, and she knew from watching them leave earlier that they had nothing but their guns and the clothing they were wearing. All their other gear was in the saddlebags they'd stowed in the barn when they decided to stay. But knowing Gareth's determination and recklessness, Vicky wasn't betting on him giving up just to avoid discomfort. He was the obsessive type once he set his mind to something, and right now, she was afraid she was the target of that obsession, the one thing in the world he was zeroed in on. Thinking of that chilled her as surely as the dropping temperature.

The slope continued to steepen, and Vicky decided to dismount and lead Tucker from that point forward. It was much safer that way anyway, both for her and the horse, as it would be far too easy for him to slip and break a leg among the rocks. She gave him a gentle pat and whispered to him that he was in good hands now and that they would get out of here, but she wondered if she could keep that promise. If it came down to having to leave him and climb out in order to escape, Vicky told herself she would do so and find a place to hide out and wait for Eric. He would help her get all three of the horses back, and then he would rid her grandpa's property of Gareth, Jeremy and Brett, one way or the other.

She came to the end of the line for Tucker sooner than she expected. The only way forward, other than going back down to the stream bed far below, was a scramble across a steep talus field that would be impossible for a horse. Vicky would have to use both hands and feet to safely traverse it, and Tucker couldn't follow. "I'm going to have to leave you here for now, boy," She whispered to the horse. You can wait, or you can go back to the barn. I won't tie you up, but I've got to keep going." She patted him again and drew the reins up tighter behind his neck, so he wouldn't snag them on the underbrush, and then she began scrambling across. Once she reached the other side of the boulders that had piled up after sliding down from somewhere on the walls above, she found herself out in the open, on another shelf. To her left was a steep drop off into the canyon, and to her right were unclimbable cliffs reaching to the rim. She couldn't go up or down, only forward, up towards the head of the dead-end canyon. Vicky hoped she could find the way out once she got there, but she'd only seen that part of the canyon from below, where the waterfalls were. Her grandpa had told her that a person could climb out, but she didn't know the exact route. She had to find it before dark or else find a place to hide, and she wondered now if she should turn back and work her way down among the trees to do so. She looked back to see if she could still see Tucker and saw to her dismay that she was too late. Gareth was emerging from the forest at the edge of the boulder field, and he'd already seen her and was bringing her grandfather's rifle to his shoulder.

ERIC PLACED BOB BARHAM'S HAT OVER HIS FACE AND picked up his rifle, handing it to Shauna, who was standing there quietly with tears streaming down her face. The old man had been kind to her and Jonathan; one of the few truly good people they'd met on their dangerous odyssey. Bob had been willing to drop everything he was doing for them and share all that he had to help them find Megan. It was unfair that he died in such a meaningless way, but Eric knew there wasn't much that was fair any more. Unfortunately, the fallen Appaloosa horse that Bob had been attempting to help wasn't going to make it either. Eric still didn't know who shot it, but he figured it was either Jeremy or Brett. He'd get to the bottom of that later after he found Vicky. The bullet that hit the horse had apparently nicked an artery. It had managed to run for a while, but now it had lost too much blood and wasn't getting back up. Frightened and in pain, it was slowly expiring on the blood-spattered pine needles on the ground around it.

"Poor baby," Shauna said. "He's suffering, isn't he? We can't just leave him like this!"

"I'll take care of it while you get the others ready to ride," Eric said, drawing his knife. "There's nothing else that can be done. And we'll take Bob's body back to his property when we go back there for Jonathan. I'm sure he'd rather be buried there on his own land."

That settled, they were riding south out of the pines and across the open pasture lands of the ranch just minutes later. Eric had left Bob's loaded packhorse and the horse Shauna had run down tethered to a tree. He'd also left Brett there, bound with Bob's lasso. Leaving Brett there was partly for insurance against Jeremy trying to break and run. It would also be easier to keep up with just one of them and Jeremy was the one who'd been with Gareth when Vicky was seen. Jeremy was also the one that shot Bob, and it might have done him good to have to sit there tied up with Brett near the body, contemplating what he'd done, but Eric needed him right now. And besides, it wasn't about punishment, at least not yet. The kid's story was believable anyway, and Eric didn't really think it was cold-blooded murder. It was probably a panicked reaction, just as he'd explained it, but it was certainly unfortunate for Bob.

The main thing he wanted from these two young men and their other companion that was pursuing Vicky was information. They'd set out after Megan when she left but had failed to catch up to her. Eric wanted to know why, and he wanted to know every little detail that led to them arriving back here today. It would have to wait a little longer though, because getting to Vicky was top priority for the moment. As they rode off, he and Shauna on the horses they'd ridden here on with Bob, and Jeremy leading the way just ahead of them on Bob's own mount, Eric glanced over his shoulders at Brett, helplessly lashed to the tree where he'd left him. Eric figured by the time they returned and cut him loose, probably after dark, his memory of the things Eric wanted to know about might feel a little fresher.

As the three of them rode in the direction of the canyon where Jeremy said Vicky had gone, Eric thought of all that had changed for him and Shauna with the single shot that killed Bob Barham. Eric had only known the man for a few hours, but it had been clear that he had a wealth of first-hand knowledge to share about these mountains, and that he was willing to share both that knowledge and his time to help Eric and Shauna in their quest. Now he was gone, but Eric knew the old man would still want them to make use of his horses and gear. Shauna would agree when they talked about it later, as it was really the only option they had. Eric already knew that Bob lived alone and had no one else depending on him, and because of that, there was no one else to take care of the animals anyway. While he hadn't been completely comfortable with the idea of Bob going along with them just hours ago when they first discussed it, the fact was that they were *his* horses and he didn't want to sell any of them. After riding here with him from the place where they'd met though, Eric felt a little better about it. Bob fancied himself a mountain man or cowboy in the mold of the pioneers that first settled this land. While he was perhaps a hundred and fifty years too late to live that kind of life, Eric could tell that Bob had spent a lot of time and effort trying to recreate it anyway, even if only part-time. The survival skills he'd acquired would have served him well in the present circumstances, but now it didn't matter because he'd been gunned down without a fight, simply because he'd had a rifle in his hand. Eric knew it could have happened to anyone, but regardless of the circumstances of his death, Eric felt sad for the old man. He'd been so excited on the way here, as he was about to embark on a great mountain journey on horseback; a wilderness trek like the heroes he emulated had routinely made in the days he'd dreamed of living. Now it was over for him, but Bob Barham had died in the mountains he loved, having spent all of his last day riding his beloved Ginny on the trail. Eric figured it was as good a death as most men could hope for. He would take Bob back to his own place and give him a proper burial, the least he could do for a man who'd taken in his ex-wife and friend, offering all he had.

If the two men he'd found at the scene hadn't been frantically bent over Bob, freaking out and trying to stop his bleeding, Eric would have wasted them without hesitation. But the look on their faces, and their obvious youth stayed his trigger finger, and he was glad of it now. Whatever they could tell him was worth far more than

SCOTT B. WILLIAMS

making them pay for their mistakes. Eric wasn't in the business of dealing out sentences for wrongdoing, at least not when he wasn't getting paid for it or it wasn't a clear case of someone attacking a helpless victim, like the two he'd taken out on that Louisiana road after they'd pulled a young mother out of her car. Eric's only concern here was getting to Vicky before Gareth did. *He* was the one who'd been his daughter's boyfriend, and Eric intended to have a nice, long chat with that one. What would come afterward depended on how that conversation went. But no matter where it led him, Eric had made a promise to Vicky that he wouldn't leave her behind, and he had every intention of keeping it.

The open pasture lands they were crossing rose in a gradual slope as they neared the far side, and Jeremy led the way to the bed of a small stream, saying it was the one that wound its way down out of the canyon where Vicky was seen. "Gareth and I were up there," Jeremy said, pointing to a steep ridge overlooking the drainage. "He saw her heading up into it, and he said there's no way to ride out of there once you get farther into the canyon."

"Have you been there before?" Eric asked.

"No, not all the way, but Gareth has. He wanted me and Brett to come back and wait out here, in case she tried to slip back out and head for the road. I don't know that she already hasn't, but the last he saw of her she was heading farther up the creek, in the woods along that slope over there." Jeremy pointed at the western side of the drainage. "Gareth said it was too steep to take a horse much farther up there though. If she didn't manage to get out, she might have left it behind. It's one of those spotted Appaloosas like the other two."

"Listen carefully to me, Jeremy," Eric said. "I should probably tie you up like your friend, but I know you're not going to try anything, because if you do, my ex-wife will shoot you dead before you finish the thought. If you doubt it, let me assure you that you won't be the first dude she's shot lately." Eric's expression was matter-of-fact; completely devoid of emotion, and when he watched Jeremy glance over at Shauna as if to confirm this was true, Eric saw that hers was just as icy. The message got through. Jeremy nodded that he understood, and Eric turned to Shauna.

"You're okay with this, right baby?" He didn't know why he called her that. It just came out, but Shauna didn't seem to mind. "You've got your rifle if anything happens. I'm heading in there to see if I can find them."

Shauna agreed, and Eric ordered Jeremy to dismount. Shauna climbed down from the saddle herself and tied her horse to a bush at the edge of the tree line. Eric gave her a hug. "I hate to split up again so soon, but I'm counting on being back quick. I really need you here for the same reason that Gareth wanted his two buddies here. If either Vicky or Gareth comes out of there all of a sudden, you'll at least have a chance of heading them off."

"Be careful, Eric." She put her hand around his neck

and pulled his face to hers, planting a kiss on his lips. It was brief, but nice, like the one before he left on that mission for Lieutenant Holton. Eric didn't know what to make of it, but he didn't mind it a bit. He swung back up in the saddle with a smile, already feeling more at home with this riding stuff even though he'd been at it less than a day. But Eric didn't plan to just ride up into that canyon where he could be easily spotted. He knew Gareth had a deer rifle and that he'd fired at a buck from one of the slopes above. The guy might shoot at him on sight, even though he wouldn't have a clue who Eric was or why he was here. He used the horse to save time closing the gap, riding it only until he reached the area Jeremy had pointed out, and then he dismounted and left it waiting, striking out through the woods on foot in the direction Jeremy thought Vicky had traveled.

Eric was cautious, but he was in a hurry too. It was nearly sundown now and he knew that finding anyone in this terrain after dark wouldn't be easy. As he entered a dense grove of spruce trees after climbing up out of the creek bottom on the other side, Eric discovered there was really only one logical route leading up the canyon. It was a natural shelf with an almost path-like appearance, and he figured it was probably a game trail used by deer and other large animals going back and forth through the drainage since the undergrowth down lower was too dense and the slope became a cliff higher up. So Eric followed it, thinking it the most likely route Vicky would have taken, especially if she were still riding. His hunch

was confirmed when he came across fresh horse drop-
pings directly in his path. Seeing that, he quickened his
pace, knowing he was on the right track, and shortly
after, he spotted a horse. It had the distinct markings of
an Appaloosa, just as Jeremy had said, and it was
standing there looking at him with little concern, tied to a
bush by the reins, but wearing no saddle, which
confirmed Brett's earlier story. There was no sign of
Vicky or Gareth nearby, so Eric approached the horse
slowly, quietly whispering to it in a soothing voice to
keep it quiet, while watching the cover for signs of movement. He quickly determined that any possible route
beyond this point was decidedly treacherous and steep,
and Eric concluded that Vicky had continued on foot
because it was her only choice. The only question was
whether Gareth had come this way too, and how far
behind her he might be. Eric got his answer when the
crack of a high-powered rifle echoed through the canyon
just ahead. The sound made the horse skittish and he
pulled at the reins and pawed the ground. Eric ignored
him and moved carefully in the direction of the sound,
his M4 at ready as he looked for the best route across the
boulders that lay in his way.

SEVEN

WHEN JEREMY LEFT TO GO BACK FOR BRETT AND the other horses, Gareth took off down the slope to the creek at a run, leaping from rock to rock at a reckless pace to reach the stream bed as quickly as possible. When he was at the bottom, he splashed through it in the same place he'd seen the deer and horse cross, and then he was climbing uphill again, picking his way through the dense spruce grove that covered the opposite slope.

Gareth was *pissed!* He was furious that Brett had failed the one simple task he'd given him—to watch the horses while they went hunting—and he was pissed that Vicky had taken his favorite of the three Appaloosas. If he hadn't spotted her by chance when he did, he knew he might never have found her. Why she had headed into the canyon though, he wasn't sure, as it seemed like she would have taken the road or one of the main trails out if she wanted to cover a lot of ground and ensure her escape. Gareth smiled as he thought of the trap she had ridden into. *Maybe Vicky didn't know it was a box canyon?* The old man had shown it to Gareth and Aaron, but that didn't mean he'd ever taken his granddaughter there. As long as he could prevent her from turning around and riding back out, Gareth was certain that he could catch her in this place, and he smiled as he thought of all the ways he might make her pay for doing this to him. He'd already been thinking about Vicky a lot ever since he made the decision to come back here. He had liked her well enough when the three of them began to hang out together, which was often, considering that she was Megan's roommate back then. She wasn't as hot as Megan, but then no one he'd ever dated had been. But if Megan hadn't been in the picture, Vicky would have been fair game, and now, she definitely was. Back in the beginning, she'd liked him too. He could see it in the way she looked at him. He knew she was a little jealous of Megan, because some dude she'd been head over heels in love with had dumped her hard. Gareth could have had her easily back then, but then after all the action started and they left town for the mountains, Vicky didn't like the direction things were going. In fact, she'd become a real pain in Gareth's ass, and he figured her running her mouth so much was the main reason Megan wouldn't get on board completely with the resistance. And of course, it was Vicky's idea to come here to this ranch in the first place; her idea being to hide from the world until it was all made better again, which Gareth knew was delusional thinking. It wouldn't be made better until there was a purging, and that purging was going to require a lot of blood. Why everyone else couldn't see that was beyond Gareth's comprehension.

Being involved with Megan may have derailed him temporarily, but that was absolutely over now. After what he'd seen out there in the mountains, he was quite sure she and Aaron never made it through, and that they were both likely dead by now. Gareth had come back here to think and to resupply. The latter wasn't going to happen now, but he could still do the thinking and planning. Brett and Jeremy would follow him anywhere, he just had to decide where to go to try and find more like-minded people to join up with and help keep the momentum going while the authorities were still trying to catch up. But without all three of the horses, they were screwed, and Gareth was determined not to lose the one he'd seen that bitch riding away on. He didn't want to have to kill her outright, but if there was no other way to stop her, then he would do what was necessary.

As he made his way through the spruce trees, climbing higher up the slope, Gareth stumbled upon clear evidence that he was on Vicky's trail. He had been watching out for tracks, as the one thing that stuck with him from all the times he'd hunted with Aaron was the importance of looking at the ground. Aaron was really good at tracking and could tell from the subtlest sign about how long ago an animal or person had passed by, finding indications that most people would never notice. Gareth knew nothing of that, but he knew what fresh horse shit looked like when he saw it, especially when he stepped in it and got it smeared all over his boots. Grinning as he scraped the soles against a tree root to wipe it away, Gareth paused for a moment to dig more rifle cartridges out of his pocket, shoving three fresh ones into the Winchester's magazine to replace the ones he'd fired.

The drainage was like a natural funnel with only a couple of reasonable ways in or out. Vicky had taken the only possible path a horse could negotiate on this side of the canyon. She had to either keep going or else turn around and go back down to the creek and follow it up, but if she tried that, she would run right into him. Gareth pressed on, confident that he would soon have her cornered when she reached the point where there were no more options. He couldn't see back down to the creek from where he was now in the forest, but he hoped that Jeremy and Brett would soon have his back and be there waiting and ready in case Vicky somehow found a way to elude him and make for the pastures and the road beyond.

When he reached a place where the woods opened up and the ground became rockier and steeper, Gareth spotted movement among the trees up ahead and stopped to raise his rifle, so he could use the scope. *It was Tucker, the horse she'd taken, standing there by himself, looking back at him!* Gareth moved the crosshairs slowly beyond the horse to an open area of boulders that covered the slope, creating an obstacle that Tucker couldn't cross. Vicky was nowhere in sight, and he was sure she had continued across the rocks on foot, as it was the only way she could have gone without him seeing her. He approached Tucker and tied the reins to a branch. He was going to need him on the way back and he didn't want him to get away. "Just hang tight, Tucker. I'll be back for you before long," Gareth whispered. "I know the last thing you wanted to do was come running off up here this late in the afternoon after all the riding we've been doing. You'll get a break after this though, I promise."

Just as he emerged from the woods and began looking for the best route across the boulders, Gareth spotted something moving on the other side, and once again raised his rifle to use the scope. *It was Vicky!* She had seen him though, and already disappeared around the rock face to her right a second after he had her in focus. Gareth had to shoulder the rifle on its sling in order to pursue her further. The boulder-strewn slope was a serious obstacle that required his full attention to traverse without twisting an ankle or worse, and he often had to use his hands as well as both feet to climb up and over the larger ones. He'd just reached the edge of them and was studying the only possible route forward when he saw movement again, this time nearly two hundred yards farther ahead and higher, on a ledge that formed a natural path to the head of the canyon. Gareth steadied himself and raised the rifle to get another look through the scope. He knew it was her, even before he leveled the crosshairs on her face. Vicky had seen him again too and was looking right at him for a second before she turned away, trying to duck from his view. He could see that she was carrying a rifle, and that it looked like the .22 Magnum that Brett had been using, which made sense, because Brett had been the one guarding the horses. Gareth was really pissed at Brett now, and figured he must have totally fallen asleep on the job, in order for this girl to sneak up like that and steal not only the horse, but his weapon too. If she did that, she could have killed the dumbass as well if she'd wanted to, but Gareth doubted she had it in her. Even so, she was armed, so he knew he had to be careful. But he hoped she'd give up now that she knew she was trapped. Gareth moved his aim point a bit farther up, putting the crosshairs on the rock face some ten feet above her head. He was tired of this chase now and he was ready for her to stop. He hoped as he pulled the trigger that a bullet slamming into rock that close would get her attention and make her realize that the game was up.

But Vicky didn't stop. Instead, she ducked low behind another rock and pointed the rifle back his way. It was a long shot for a .22 Magnum, but Gareth wasn't taking any chances. He dropped low among the boulders and waited, expecting an incoming round any moment.

When it didn't happen, he raised his head just enough to see and could tell she was still behind the rock. Gareth waited a moment more and when she still didn't shoot, he brought his scope back up to his eye to get a closer look. He could see her now, fumbling with the rifle, working the bolt, and looking confused. Then he broke out into a laugh. Brett was such an idiot that he'd left the rifle unloaded when they'd all sat around cleaning their guns and taking inventory of the rounds they had left after eating the two MREs they found in the barn. He wasn't planning on going hunting with them, so he didn't refill the tubular magazine with the cartridges he'd taken out and put in his pocket. It was funny now, thinking about how Vicky must be feeling.

Gareth stood up and walked right towards her, the rifle at his hip and pointed in her direction. There was nowhere to run to that she could reach before he shot her, and she had to be aware of that. When he was halfway there, she stood up from behind her cover and placed the useless rifle on the waist-high chunk of rock in front of her. She was going to make it easy for him, and Gareth smiled with relief.

"I didn't think you really wanted to shoot me, Vicky," he called out as he walked closer, lowering the muzzle of his rifle as he did. "I don't know why you took off like that anyway. I was looking forward to seeing you again when I got here. I was worried something had happened to you when we found the house burned down... and your grandparents buried out there..." Vicky didn't answer, so Gareth kept walking closer, talking all the while. "I'm sorry about whatever happened to them, but we're gonna all get out of here, Vicky. We'll make a good team, you and me. Megan was just a big mistake. I know that now, and I know it was you I should have been hanging with all along."

Vicky still didn't react, even to that. Gareth kept closing in until he was only 20 feet away from where she stood behind that rock, her face expressionless as she watched him. It was as if she wasn't even hearing what he was saying. But then suddenly, her hand came up and in the next moment she was pointing a black semi-automatic pistol directly at him, locking it down with a two-handed grip. He hadn't expected her to have a handgun on her too, but figured it was one of her grandfather's that she may have had on her when she escaped whoever raided the ranch.

"Don't take another step, Gareth! Put my grandpa's rifle down and turn around and go back the way you came!"

"Seriously, Vicky? You're threatening me with a gun?"

"I *will* shoot you, Gareth Mabry! You stole from us and you've already shot at me twice today!"

"I wasn't shooting *at* you Vicky, or I would have hit you. I thought you'd have enough sense to stop. Now quit this nonsense, or I *will* have to shoot you!"

"I'm not bluffing, Gareth. PUT. THE. RIFLE. DOWN!"

Gareth looked at her with a smirk. Did she really think he was that much of a pushover? He slowly raised the rifle to his shoulder, bringing it in line with her upper body. But before he could utter another word, he felt a sensation like hot needles burning through his chest, taking his breath away. For a split second, it made no sense, until his brain processed the barking reports from the pistol, and he saw the arc of spent shell casings spinning away from Vicky's hands. Time seemed to switch to a kind of weird slow motion for Gareth as he first sank to his knees, still staring at Vicky, the last thing he saw before everything went black when his face slammed into the hard granite in front of him.

VICKY WASN'T REALLY AWARE OF HOW MANY TIMES she'd fired the Glock. She just pulled the trigger over and over, trying to keep it on target until Gareth was no longer standing. She was surprised at how quickly he'd gone down, and surprised that she'd apparently hit him with most of her rounds. Vicky didn't trust him for a second, and when he raised the rifle she acted without hesitation. Before her grandparents were killed, Vicky couldn't really imagine taking another person's life, but now that she knew there were those who would readily kill anyone weaker or caught off guard, Vicky's entire mindset had changed. Even before she realized that the rifle she'd taken back from Brett was unloaded, Vicky had made up her mind that she would kill Gareth if he pushed her far enough. She'd already thought too that it would be better if she did, because even if he turned around and walked away if she threatened him, she wouldn't trust that he would actually leave. She knew now that he was a genuinely bad person, and that he would stop at nothing to get what he wanted or needed to survive. She had hoped she could escape and evade him until Eric returned, but that had proven impossible. If she'd attempted to continue climbing out of the canyon, she would have made herself an easy target for Gareth or perhaps even fallen to her death as it was getting too dark to pick a safe route up those steep rocks.

Vicky's hands were shaking hard now, even though she'd managed to control them when she was actually shooting. She still had both of them wrapped around the grip of the Glock, and she kept it pointed in Gareth's general direction until she was certain he was down for good. But even in the fading light, she could see the blood spreading on the stone surface beneath his body, which was unmoving. Vicky would have to walk right by him to get back to where she'd left Tucker, and she knew she couldn't wait any longer if she wanted to ride out of the drainage before dark. Gareth had fallen on top of the deer rifle, but Vicky was determined to retrieve it, not only because it was her grandpa's, but because she didn't know where Jeremy was or even that Brett hadn't made his way out here to join in the search for her. The answer seemed to come, and her heart nearly stopped when she heard someone shout her name from the direction both she and Gareth had come. But then she saw that it wasn't Jeremy or Brett. The man calling out to her was Eric Branson. He was waving at her now and he repeated his name again to make sure she recognized him. Vicky left the rifle where it was under Gareth and backed away to wait for him to get there.

"Are you okay, Vicky? Are you hurt?"

"No, I'm fine," she said, holding the Glock down at her side now, pointed at the ground. "I didn't want this to happen," she said, glancing at Gareth's body, and then back at Eric as she struggled with the words to explain.

"It's okay, Vicky. You did what you had to do, and I'm glad you were able to. I take it that's Gareth, right?"

"Yes! He was chasing me. He already shot at me from somewhere on the other side of the creek when I was riding down there on Tucker. I was sure he was going to kill me just now. I tried to get him to put down the rifle, but he wouldn't do it."

"I know, Vicky. You don't have to explain."

"I didn't think anyone would help me. I had no idea you'd be back so soon. Or that you would look for me here."

"I found horses faster than I expected, Vicky. But I also found Gareth's friends, Brett and Jeremy. They told me you were up here, and that Gareth had gone after you. I came as fast as I could, but I would have been too late. I'm glad you were able to use that," Eric said, nodding at the Glock.

Vicky suddenly remembered who it belonged to, and handed it to him butt first, taking care not to point the barrel back at herself as she did so. She watched as he swapped out the magazine for a full one, and then returned it to his carry position inside his belt. She couldn't watch though when he squatted down beside Gareth's body to check for vital signs.

"He's gone, isn't he?" She asked when Eric stood.

"Yes. You did well. It was quick."

"I didn't really want to kill him, but I had to stop him!"

"It was the right thing to do, Vicky. From what little I've learned of him since I got here, he couldn't be trusted. There were some questions I wanted to ask him, but maybe his two buddies can answer most of them."

"I thought they were after me too and when I heard you call my name, I thought it was Jeremy." Vicky became nervous again, glancing back over Eric's shoulders. "They're still out there somewhere! We'd better be careful!"

"Nope, you don't have to worry about either of them, Vicky. Megan's mom is keeping a close eye on Jeremy, and Brett isn't going anywhere until I cut him loose. You are completely safe now, and the horse you were riding is waiting for you just back there in the woods."

That was a lot to process, and now Vicky was really confused. Eric had mentioned that Megan's mother was supposed to be heading to the ranch, and that he'd expected her to be here when he arrived yesterday, but

Vicky had seen no one else here since the place was attacked.

"I'll explain it all later," Eric said. "Let's get down out of here before it gets dark. Shauna must have heard all the shooting and she's going to be wondering what happened.

EIGHT

E{RIC WASN'T PARTICULARLY HAPPY ABOUT FINDING} Gareth Mabry dead, but he didn't want to make Vicky feel bad about it either. She had done well to defend herself against him and had come out the victor in a close-range armed encounter, which was an accomplishment for anyone, even those with training and experience. Eric had been prepared to kill Gareth himself if necessary, to protect Vicky, of course, but he'd *really* wanted to talk to the young man if at all possible. He was sure that Gareth could have told him more about Megan than anyone else he could ask here in Colorado, even her former roommate. Megan had been romantically involved with him (according to Vicky) at least for a time, and Gareth surely knew what she'd been thinking, and what she'd wanted to do when things began deteriorating around them. But Gareth was dead now, and that was that. Eric would have to find his answers elsewhere.

Considering all that had happened, he figured he was lucky to have Vicky, Jeremy and Brett to question. Vicky would be going south with him, of course, so there would be plenty of time to talk with her. Jeremy and Brett however, most certainly were not, and Eric had to get their story quickly because there was little time to waste. They untied Vicky's horse from where Gareth had left it and led it down to the creek bed to find Eric's. It was dark and getting cold fast, but they found Shauna and Jeremy waiting where they were supposed to be. Eric introduced the two women and informed Jeremy that his friend was dead.

"We'll go back and get Brett and the other two horses and then go back to the barn for the night."

"What about Bob?" Shauna asked. "We can't leave him out there all night. The coyotes and other animals will find him for sure."

"We'll put him on one of the horses then and bring him back to the barn too. We can redistribute stuff from his packhorse in the morning since we have an extra horse now. It won't be a problem to take him back to his cabin for burial."

Jeremy said little during the ride back to where they'd left Brett. He was visibly shaken though when Eric and Vicky came back without Gareth, and Eric thought that was a good thing. The boy knew without question he meant business, and hopefully, he and Brett would talk freely now that they had no fear of repercussions from their ringleader. Both of them were probably scared to death, wondering what he was going to do to them for killing Bob. They had to have seen enough by now to know that justice was in the hands of whoever had the guns, and that it was being meted out far more swiftly and efficiently than at any time in recent history. He didn't want them to know it, but Eric had already made up his mind he wasn't going to punish them directly for shooting Bob. Eric believed that Jeremy shot him out of fear for his own life. Eric knew they were all thieves, and Gareth had paid the ultimate price for their decision to come back here to steal yet again. The other two would probably pay it too soon enough, simply because they didn't have the means or the skills necessary to survive out here. What happened to them after they were left here without the stolen horses and guns wasn't Eric's problem, and he would make that clear to them when he was done with his questions later.

It was cold, and they were all tired by the time they arrived at the barn more than an hour later, but no one was going to sleep until they were done talking, and Eric had his answers. Eric busted up some of the planking boards from one side of the old structure to build a fire outside the gate. He didn't care what happened to the barn after tonight; the boys could stay and use it for shelter or not, but he was going to burn all the wood he needed to have a fire so they could comfortably sit and talk.

"We can start from the beginning, because Shauna hasn't heard any of this except the few bits and pieces I told her on the way here today with Bob. I want to know everything that happened since you all left Boulder," Eric said, including Vicky in his questioning. "I especially want to know why Megan left this ranch when it was still relatively safe here and there was plenty of food to go around. Why would she take off alone with Aaron like that? And what did Gareth do in the first place to cause her to break up with him if they were so wrapped up in each other when all of you left the campus?"

It took a lot of back and forth and roundabout questioning to get it out of them, but Jeremy and Brett knew exactly why Megan had come to be disgusted with Gareth. The more time she spent with him, the more she learned who he really was. Gareth had already been involved in more troublemaking activity than she knew about when she first went with him to that resistance camp. He'd bragged about the details of some of those actions to Jeremy and Brett to impress them, but when he later opened up to Megan and told her more over time, her reaction was opposite what he'd hoped. She was horrified that he was capable of such things, and especially that he wanted to do even more if he could find another group to join. By the time she'd learned all this, she had already gotten to know Aaron and was drawn to him because his motivation was only to survive and find peace; quite the opposite of Gareth. Most of their story matched what Vicky had already told Eric about Megan and Aaron, and why Megan went with him, though even Vicky was learning new things about

Gareth too as Brett and Jeremy kept talking, especially when they described what happened after they and Colleen left with him.

"So, you're telling me that you agreed to let Gareth use your girlfriend as bait?" Eric asked Brett. "You agreed to put Colleen in that kind of danger?"

"I didn't like it but yeah, it seemed like it would work. And besides, Colleen wanted to do it. She thought we could get away with it. She thought Gareth's plan was brilliant."

"It didn't occur to any of you that it would turn out exactly like it did?" Eric asked. "If you weren't prepared to fight those guys, why would you attempt to steal from them like that?"

"We just thought they would believe her. All we wanted to do was divide them up. Gareth said they'd probably all go with her when they heard Colleen's story. He said they might leave one to guard the stuff, but that we could deal with him."

"But instead, they never let Colleen leave at all. Instead, they came looking for you, trying to hunt you down. Imagine that! And you three hauled ass and bailed on her, leaving her in the hands of a bunch of strangers. You didn't even *try* to get her back! How did that make you feel, Brett? She was *your* girlfriend!"

"I felt like shit! Believe me! But we couldn't fight all those guys with the kinds of weapons they had. We had no choice but to get out of there. The only reason we got away was because we had the horses. We went days out of our way to avoid them before coming back here and we weren't even sure we'd ever be able to find the place until we just happened upon the main trail again. We didn't have any other choice but to come back for more supplies. I was planning to go back and look for her later, but we weren't expecting to find what we found when we got here. I swear man!"

Eric took all of this in, piecing together the scenario as he thought how it might have played out. He was so glad now that Megan had the good sense to get the hell away from Gareth when she did, even if he didn't know where she was. And he was glad Gareth was dead. The guy was a total sociopath with no regard for others.

"I guess none of you considered that those folks you sent Colleen to all alone would have a way to make her talk, did you? And that she would tell them what you two and Gareth were all about, and what you'd been doing since the riots started? I guess you didn't consider that she might tell them where you all came from, or that they would come here too, looking for you? And when they did, they would find an isolated house stockpiled with goods, as well as more horses in the pasture? And that there would be no one here to guard it but an old man and woman and their granddaughter; people who had sheltered and supported the three terrorists that you had become?"

"No!" Jeremy insisted. "Who *would* think of all that? We just needed supplies, so we wouldn't starve out here! After we lost everything in the rapids, we were desperate! Hunting for all our food wasn't going to work. Aaron could do it, but he'd been doing it all his life. We found out we couldn't hunt *and* cover any kind of distance at the same time. That's not as easy as Aaron made it look! But the main reason we came back is because of those guys. They looked like some kind of militia-type dudes getting ready to start a war."

"Then it was a bad judgment call to try and steal from them, wasn't it? And even dumber to send Colleen out to them alone?"

"Like I said, it was *Gareth's* idea! Yeah, it was dumb, but we didn't expect it to turn out like it did."

"I see. But what I don't understand, Jeremy, is why you and Brett were so eager to help Gareth find my daughter anyway. You knew she didn't want to have anything else to do with him. Did any of you think she was going to change her mind just because you followed her to where she was going with Aaron?"

"That part wasn't any of our business," Jeremy said. "That was between Gareth and Megan. We went along with him because we're his friends, and he'd do the same for us. He was going to leave anyway, so there wasn't any reason for me and Brett to hang around here. What would we do here anyway?"

"What you could have done—*should* have done—was stay here and help that old man and woman that opened up their home and ranch for all of you. Instead, you took his horses and guns and not only left him without help but brought down the wrath of even worse people you tried to deceive and rob."

"I know we screwed up," Brett said. "We probably shouldn't have listened to Gareth, but he had a way of making you see things his way. It worked on your daughter too, man, I hate to tell you! She may have seen through his shit and dumped him in the end, but she believed every word he told her in the beginning. The dude was slick, man!"

Hearing the description of the group Jeremy and Brett described, Eric considered that they probably were part of some larger movement or organization, possibly militia of one persuasion or another, but the fact that they held Colleen and did no telling what with her afterward meant that they certainly weren't the good guys. Eric thought back to the group he'd rescued Sergeant Connelly from and figured there were militia cells like that springing up everywhere. Down there in the south, the lakeshores, rivers and swamps tended to be the places farthest from roads where they could organize and operate. Out here, it was the rugged high country of the mountains that they would claim as their strongholds. The group these guys had encountered were well equipped to operate in the backcountry, and from the description of their tents and other gear, Eric figured most of them were locals to the region and probably expert hunters and backwoodsmen. It was a wonder Gareth and his two buddies escaped them at all. Of course there was no proof that the men that had Colleen were the same that came here and attacked the ranch, but it certainly seemed to fit. As the story came to light under Eric's questioning, Vicky especially believed that to be the case. Brett had told her something completely different regarding Colleen's disappearance, but now that she had this version, her anger at him had grown exponentially. When she told him to his face that she wished she'd just shot him that afternoon when she had a chance, Eric believed her.

"I feel bad for Colleen," Vicky said, "even if she was in on stealing the horses and stuff here, they talked her into it. Then they tricked her into doing something stupid and did nothing to try and save her. Maybe we can find her? Jeremy and Brett can tell us exactly where it happened, and it must be on our way when we go after Megan and Aaron anyway."

"They may be able to tell us where it happened, Vicky, but I think it's unlikely those guys are still in the same place. Especially if they really were the ones that attacked this place. We'll keep an eye out for them, for sure though, because if they *are* part of a larger organization, it could make our trip much more difficult than we thought." He turned to Shauna. "You said Bob had loads of topographic maps in his cabin, right? Maps that we may be able to use to pick an alternate route?"

"Yes, he showed them to me. He's got detailed back-country maps that cover all of Colorado and most of New Mexico, Wyoming and Montana. He said he had always dreamed of a horseback trip along the entire

Continental Divide. He had a lot of books about it in his cabin as well. But if we know Megan and Aaron were planning to use the Continental Divide Trail, shouldn't we stick with it, in case we catch up to them somewhere along the way?"

"It's not likely we would," Eric said. "They had a good head start and they are traveling on horseback too. It sounds like Aaron knows what he is doing and they left well-supplied. If they got through without encountering any trouble, then we won't catch them before they get to where they're going. If they did have to divert to another route to avoid some danger, then it won't matter anyway. They could be anywhere out there. All we can do is get to what we know was their planned destination and work back from there if we don't find them. I hope it doesn't come to that, but at least if we have all of Bob's maps, we'll be able to see all the options they may have used."

Eric looked at Brett and Jeremy again. There probably wasn't a whole lot more they could tell him. He felt truly sorry for the girl, but like he'd told Vicky, he doubted they'd ever find her even if she were the main focus of their search. And he knew full well she may not even be alive. Gareth's ruse might have worked if he and his two companions had the balls to back it up, but they'd cut and run, sealing her fate. From the way Jeremy and Brett described it, the camp they intended to rob wasn't far from a gravel forest service road that crossed the main trail. They had seen the smoke from the campfires when they deviated off along the road to look for a place to camp themselves. After watching the men there through his riflescope for a while, Gareth had instructed Colleen to ride straight into the camp from that road with a story about how she and her sister were coming around a curve a few miles back on the road in their dead father's truck, but had swerved to miss a deer and got the horse trailer they were pulling stuck in the ditch. They couldn't pull it out, but she'd unloaded one of the two horses to go looking for help and she'd seen their campfires. She was to tell the men that she and her sister had been heading to their family's vacation cabin after their father died at their home in Pueblo, and that the truck was loaded down with the supplies they would need to spend the winter there, where it was safe. Gareth's thinking was that if she told them that she thought the men with their ATVs could get the trailer back up onto the road, then they would either go along, sincerely wanting to help, or pretend to, while actually planning to steal whatever was in the truck and take the two girls. Either way, if most or all of them left, Gareth, Jeremy and Brett would be waiting in hiding near the camp, and when the men were gone, they would swoop in and load all the supplies on their horses as fast as they could and then meet Colleen after she took off on her horse through the woods where the ATVs couldn't follow.

The problem with their plan was that the three would-be raiders didn't know how to do proper reconnaissance and they had seriously miscalculated what they were up against. Instead of the four men they had seen milling about the camp, the group was in fact nine strong. As soon as Colleen made contact, the others emerged from the tents and that's when Gareth also saw the kinds of weapons they were carrying. And whatever Colleen was telling them, they weren't buying it. The conversation between them seemed to go on for quite some time, but then she was grabbed and taken into a tent and that was the last that any of the three saw of her before seven heavily-armed and very serious-looking men started heading in their direction, spreading out through the woods as they came. It had been a narrow escape, only made possible because they had the horses and were willing to leave poor Colleen to whatever was in store for her with her captors.

Eric was not without sympathy for the girl, but he didn't think it likely that he'd be able to do anything about her situation now. Sure, he would check the location of that campsite if Jeremy and Brett could give him an accurate description and it was indeed along the way, but from what he had already heard, he assumed those guys were on the move, whether or not they were part of something bigger. Other than that location, there was little else that Jeremy and Brett could tell him, and Eric was getting tired, ready to get some sleep because he knew he was looking at a long day tomorrow.

"You've got two choices," he told Jeremy and Brett. "We're going to get some sleep, but I don't trust either one of you long enough to close my eyes. So, I can either shoot you both now, or you can roll over face down with your arms behind your backs, so I can tie you up, and I'll let you sleep here in the barn, out of the cold." Jeremy and Brett had no doubt that those were their only options. When they rolled over without a word, Eric got to his feet. "I thought so," he said, before leaving to get the rope.

"Are you gonna let us go tomorrow?" Brett asked.

"I'll sleep on it and let you know in the morning," Eric said as he pulled the lashings tight around Brett's wrists and then secured them to his bound ankles with a separate line. Finishing off the knots, he thought of his own recent experience with his hands lashed behind his back. These two would pull no such tricks. Eric was certain of that, as he'd made sure their wrists were clamped tightly together when he wrapped the rope. When he was done, he threw a couple big handfuls of hay over them so they'd have a chance of making it through the night without freezing to death. Shauna and Bob had been carrying wool blankets and bivy-sacks for their journey here, so Shauna and Vicky were set for sleeping warm, and Eric had his sleeping bag he'd gotten from Lieutenant Holton before beginning his journey west.

"Bob has lots of good equipment at his cabin," Shauna said, when Eric commented on the gear. "From the looks of it, I think he was pretty well-off. He had been a widower for several years, he said, and retired nearly as long too. He was living out his dreams up here in the mountains, and said it was the way he'd always wanted to live. The cabin is completely off the grid. There's not even a road leading to it. I'm not sure how many acres he owned there, but it is surrounded by a huge tract of national forest land. He said it was several miles down the drainage to the nearest road. He said he kept a truck down there parked at a neighbor's place, if you can call someone that lives nearly ten miles away a neighbor."

"Sounds like the perfect set up for times like these, but you said he was already living full time in his cabin before the shit hit the fan?" Eric asked.

"Yeah. He would have been up here either way. He didn't even really know how bad things were until I filled him in. I mean, he knew some of it, but his last trip into town for supplies was weeks ago."

"How much is left there now? Was he starting to run low again?"

"Oh no. There's a *lot!* He said he always kept the place stocked up with about six months' worth of food, because he liked being self-sufficient. It's all kinds of non-perishables, including a lot of lightweight freeze-dried backpacking stuff."

"Great!" Eric said. "We can load up all we can carry on the extra horses. That'll be one less thing we'll have to worry about."

Eric was tired, but it took a while for sleep to come. Shauna was close enough to reach over and touch, and Eric thought about their kiss earlier, when he'd left her to wait with Jeremy. She had initiated it, and it hadn't been as brief as he'd expected. He wanted more, but now was not the time. Thoughts of how things might play out between them mixed with his thoughts on all he'd learned today about his daughter. Jeremy and Brett had been able to shed some light on what these kids were thinking, especially the more radical ones like Gareth. It wasn't pleasant thinking about him being with Megan, but Eric took comfort in knowing that at least she had the good sense to dump him and leave.

NINE

Jonathan was trying to sleep but had barely closed his eyes when he sat up quickly at the sound of something walking on the front porch; something that sounded big and heavy on the creaking planking and interested in getting inside. He still couldn't move fast with his entire leg wrapped and splinted the way it was, but the pain was tolerable now and he'd learned to be careful and keep his weight on the other one. One of Bob's shotguns was beside the bunk, and Jonathan grabbed it as he sat there watching the door. He knew it was a bear again; maybe more than one this time. They showed up most evenings, making themselves at home around the place as they looked for food scraps or whatever else they could get into. Bob said they wouldn't bother anything, and he always took care to avoid throwing out anything that might attract them, but they were curious and came anyway. Jonathan didn't buy it when Bob said they were nothing to worry about. Until he saw them here, Jonathan had never seen a bear in the wild but knew what they were capable of. Every time he heard a sound he couldn't identify outside that door, he was convinced that any minute one of the bigger ones would smash through it and come straight for him. His hands were sweaty as he gripped the shotgun tightly, waiting for it to happen. Jonathan had faced a lot in the last several weeks, including incoming gunfire, but the thought of facing those teeth and claws was just too much.

He *hated* that he'd had to stay here alone while Shauna and Bob went on to the ranch to see if Megan was there. They had already waited for a few days to leave though, and he knew Shauna was anxious. The weather wasn't fit to travel for a couple of days after his accident, and Bob had taken them into his home and made Jonathan as comfortable as possible. As soon as it was clear enough to ride, Shauna wanted to go, and Jonathan said he could make it too, but Bob had insisted that staying there was best. He said the trail was rough going at times and that Jonathan would only delay his healing by trying to do too much too soon. But now he'd been here alone for two full days, and his imagination was beginning to run wild as he thought about the bears, mountain lions, wolves and no telling what else that he was only separated from by the windows and wooden door of the cabin. In his mind, they were coming for him now because they could sense that he was injured, and Jonathan knew that predators preferred injured or weakened prey. He'd always fancied himself quite the outdoorsman, unafraid of anything in the south Florida swamps and marshes, but this was a whole new world to Jonathan, who would take snakes, alligators and even sharks any day over the prospect of being mauled by a big four-legged carnivore.

He'd known when he left with Eric and Shauna that he was going to end up here in the Rockies, because that's where Megan likely was. It had been exciting to think about at first, and though bears and other dangerous wildlife crossed his mind, Jonathan hadn't worried much about it while they were on the move, even when it was just him and Shauna. The reality hit home though after he met Bob and saw all the furs and bear claws and other mountain man regalia he had and listened to his stories of them coming around the cabin. Bob seemed to enjoy Jonathan's reaction, even though he'd insisted before they left him alone there that he had nothing to fear from the black bears in these parts. Nevertheless, it was dark again, and he was still alone here. He'd hoped Shauna and Bob could make a quick trip to the ranch and back, but he knew lots of things could delay them. Bob said it was most of a day's ride just to get there, so they would be away at least one night. Now, it was looking like two though, and Jonathan figured the bear or bears outside would make their move that second night, confident they could finally break in ole Bob's cabin while he was safely away.

Jonathan listened, but now that he had the shotgun in hand, the heavy shuffling on the porch boards suddenly ceased. It was deathly quiet now, both inside and outside the cabin, and Jonathan didn't know which was worse. *Were the bears still out there, or not? Had they suddenly gone silent because they heard him stirring inside, and were now getting ready to charge in for the kill?"* Jonathan realized he was shaking, and it took a force of will to stop it. He tried what Eric recommended under stress—deep breaths to remain centered; stay in the moment—and all that other focus stuff he did. It sort of worked, but the silence remained until Jonathan heard someone call out his name and he about jumped out of his skin.

"JONATHAN! *Jonathan,* it's me. Eric!"

The voice was coming from somewhere out there in the dark, not on the porch where he knew there'd been a bear, but somewhere beyond at the edge of the woods. *But how in the hell?*

"Jonathan? Are you in there?"

"It *was* Eric's voice, impossible as that may be. He didn't know if Eric was even alive, but if he was, he damned sure wouldn't know Jonathan was here in this cabin in the middle of nowhere. Jonathan suddenly realized right then that it couldn't be the flesh and blood Eric Branson out there calling his name; *it was a freakin' ghost!"*

"Jonathan, Shauna and I are back. Don't shoot!"

"GO AWAY! YOU'RE NOT REAL! ERIC IS DEAD!"

Jonathan heard the man laugh now. Then he heard Shauna's voice: "Jonathan, Eric's not dead! He's right here with me. I found him on the way to the ranch. We made it back!"

Jonathan was still shaken up, but it *sounded* like Shauna's voice. And now he could hear the horses outside too. Was she for real? Was Eric really okay? Jonathan tentatively cracked the door just enough to see out and sure enough, there was Eric, sitting on a horse next to Shauna on hers. And just behind them was someone else. At first, Jonathan thought it had to be Bob. But now he could see that it wasn't the old man at all. It was a girl, a quite pretty girl about his age, in fact, her long brown hair pulled back behind her head in a pony-tail. *MEGAN! They found Megan!*

"No, this is Vicky," Shauna said when Jonathan stepped out, elated that Shauna's trip was such a resounding success. "Megan wasn't there anymore. Vicky was her roommate though."

Jonathan was still staring at her even after he heard what Shauna said, but then something else on one of the other horses pulled his attention away. Feet were hanging off one side of the saddle; feet wearing the thick, elk-skin moccasins that Bob Barham had stitched by hand from a bull he'd killed himself. The rest of his body was wrapped in a blanket. Jonathan was devastated. The old man had been so kind to him, and more than that, he was so cool and so knowledgeable. Jonathan had been looking forward to all he could learn from him on their planned wilderness horse packing trip. Now, he was dead, but Eric was alive and with them again. The stories they related to him once they'd all gone inside the cabin were overwhelming. Vicky's ordeal at the ranch. Eric's mission for the lieutenant and his escape and evasion and eventual journey to Colorado. And the incident with Jeremy and Brett that claimed the life of a good man.

"I would have killed both of those sons of bitches," Jonathan said.

"A part of me wanted to," Eric assured him, "but they didn't make me do it. They had already put down their weapons when I found them, and then they told me everything I wanted to know when I interrogated them. Don't you worry though. They're not out of the woods yet; quite literally."

"But you gave them supplies!"

"Just enough food from Bob's packhorse for them to walk back to a main road if they want to. They can turn themselves in to one of the official shelters if they make it, but if they choose not to, they'll probably die. Either way, they're in for a world of misery, so it's not like they're getting off easy. The main thing is that Gareth got what was coming to him. He was the dangerous one. Those two were just along for the ride."

Jonathan looked at Vicky again. He knew she wasn't proud of what she'd done, but he was damned sure proud of her. What a kick-ass chick! She did what she had to do, and she took down a killer the first time she ever fired a weapon at a living target! It would have been nothing for Eric to waste that dude, but Vicky did it by herself, before he even got a chance. Jonathan was really looking forward to getting to know her, but he was embarrassed to meet her like this. His leg had been wrapped up for days and he hadn't had a bath. He knew he had to stink, even if he didn't notice it himself, but then again, most people did these days without access to hot showers and soap. She probably wouldn't talk to him much anyway, since she was a college girl and all. But he could dream! Especially since she wasn't Megan. It would be pretty scary, taking an interest in the daughter of a dude like Eric Branson! Jonathan figured it was just as well for Gareth that he died before he met the man, especially since he went after her anyway when Megan wanted him to leave her alone.

Even though he was mostly useless with a leg he couldn't put any weight on, Jonathan wanted to help when Eric and the others began digging Bob's grave shortly after daylight the next morning. Shauna and Jonathan both thought he'd like to be buried in the small meadow just down the hill from the cabin, as it had been part of his view looking out over the valley every morning that he woke up there.

"It's beautiful here," Vicky said. "I wish my grandpa could have seen it. It's too bad he and Bob never met."

"It is a heck of a nice retreat," Eric said. "Too bad it'll

just be abandoned now, at least until someone stumbles upon it and moves in."

"Kind of like your dad's place on the Caloosa-hatchee, huh?" Jonathan said. "I'll bet there's somebody living in there."

"Maybe, but more likely it was just ransacked and looted. Maybe even burned. At least this place is hard enough to get to that anyone lucky enough to find it probably won't destroy it. They'd be stupid if they did, especially with winter coming."

"Yeah, I guess so. If Vicky really had been Megan, like I thought, then we could stay up here for the winter. There's enough food, at least if we could keep the bears out."

"You know, Jonathan, like I told you before, you're not obligated to help me any more than you already have. Finding Megan is mine and Shauna's responsibility. It's going to be rough traveling where we're going, even without a broken leg. I'll bet Bob would be happy to know you were staying here, making use of his place and all the supplies and gear he stashed here. You can hunt and fish to your heart's content up here too; have it all to yourself."

"No way, dude! I told you I wanted to help you find Megan, and I wasn't just running my mouth. I already came this far."

"I know you did, and I appreciate it, but I want you to understand that staying here may be the smarter option. That goes for Vicky too," Eric said, glancing at her and then Jonathan. "She's been through a lot already, and this trip is going to put her at risk again, that's a given. She may want to stay here with you and wait this one out. What about it, Vicky?" Eric turned to her again. "You're a local, and you know these mountains. You'll feel right at home here."

Jonathan's interest suddenly changed as he studied her face, waiting for her reaction. He *did* promise Eric that he would help him find Megan, whatever it took and wherever the quest led... but if this girl wanted to stay up here in Bob's mountain cabin... Jonathan might have to do the chivalrous thing and volunteer to look after her and keep her company. He would even find a way to overcome his fear of bears!

But his daydreams were crushed when Vicky said no. She said she felt responsible in part for Megan's plight, as it had been her idea to come out here in the first place. And she wanted to be around people—as many people as possible right now—at least as long as they were good people. "It's not that I would mind your company, Jonathan, but I think we would both get serious cabin fever stuck up here all winter when the snows come. We'd be better off sticking with Eric and Shauna and heading south. Aaron said his family land wasn't nearly as high in elevation as these parts, so winter there isn't as severe. If we can avoid the high passes and ridges, we should be able to make it through if we get going soon."

"Yeah, that sounds like a plan to me. I mean, I'm flexible though. I'm not really into snow or bears, but I'd hang here if you wanted to. But if we're all going, then I'm good to go too. I'm not worried about my leg at all. Bob said I'd be able to ride while it heals, and I will." Jonathan turned to Eric. "I won't slow you down dude, but if I do, just feel free to go on ahead, and I'll catch up when I can."

"I can't run the risk of getting separated on the trail, Jonathan. If you couldn't keep up, I'd just have to shoot you like a crippled horse."

"That's not funny, Eric!" Shauna said. "It was awful that you had to put that poor animal down yesterday."

"Yeah, I know. I'm sorry."

Jonathan had heard about the wounded horse, and he knew Eric was just trying to lighten the mood, and they all needed it. Burying Bob Barham so soon after they met him really sucked, but they got it done. Now he would rest here forever in peace, back home in the place he chose to spend his retirement apart from the rest of the world.

"He would be happy to know that his horses will be taken care of," Shauna said. "He sure loved his horses!"

"Just like my grandpa," Vicky said, a tear rolling down her cheek as she no doubt thought of those other two graves that she herself had dug so recently.

"So, what do we do now?" Jonathan asked. "Are we leaving today?"

"No," Eric said. "It'll be too late before we're ready. The first thing I want to do is take a thorough inventory of everything in that cabin. I want to know how much food there is and then figure out the best items to take; the stuff that packs the lightest but contains the most calories per pound."

"As I said before, there are lots of freeze-dried meals," Shauna said. "They weigh next to nothing."

"And tastes like nothing too," Eric said.

"Well, there's things like nuts: almonds, walnuts, and cashews, as well as peanut butter. And there's lots of jerky too, both store-bought beef jerky and venison jerky Bob made himself. Then there's cornbread and pancake mix; rice, dried beans and pasta. Canned goods too, but of course, they're heavy. He's also got plenty of tea and coffee stashed, and a half a dozen cases of whiskey."

"And cigars," Jonathan said. "He told me to help myself, as long as I didn't smoke more than one a day, so I did. There's a bunch more we can split up between us if you're into it, dude. Shauna wouldn't smoke one and I don't know about Vicky."

"No thanks," Vicky said.

After going through the food and determining that there was at least as much, and probably more than Bob estimated, Eric wanted to look through his other gear, including his weapons and ammo.

"He was into all this cool mountain man stuff," Jonathan said. "Check out these flintlock rifles! He showed me how they work, and he even let me shoot one of them. He said this one would kill anything that walked up here, even a grizzly bear, if they were still around."

"It probably would," Eric said, looking down the 50

caliber bore of the antique muzzleloader. "But if you didn't make that one shot count, this long barrel sure would hurt when that grizzly got through shoving it up your ass! I would suggest this one instead; it's the same caliber as that stainless steel one that Dad has on the boat." Eric was looking at Bob's Marlin .45-70. At least you've got five shots with this one, and it's a big, heavy bullet."

"Should we take it with us then? We're gonna be camping out in bear country every night on the way, aren't we?"

"Yeah, but we won't need it. We'll take the .308 that Gareth stole from Vicky's grandpa instead. It'll be more versatile for hunting or sniping duty, if we happen to have a need for either. Otherwise, we'll rely on our fighting rifles and pistols."

"I'm still sleeping with this though, no matter what." Jonathan showed him the Smith & Wesson .44 Magnum revolver that Bob kept by his bed. "It won't take up much space, but you never know man, it might come in handy. Especially since I don't have that .357 anymore."

Eric didn't argue with him and Jonathan happily put the big revolver back in his growing pile of gear. Of course, Bob had way more stuff than they could possibly carry, and it was a shame to have to leave so much of it, but it couldn't be helped. Eric wanted to carry the minimum that would see them through, and no more.

"We might as well load down all the horses and take

them," Shauna said. "We can't just abandon them here because we don't need them all."

"They'll be a liability," Eric said. "The more we take, the more we have to look out for, and keep fed and watered. And it's going to be hard enough to keep a low profile already, with four of us riding, even aside from extra packhorses."

"But you know as well as I do that these horses are as good as gold now," Eric. "You said yourself you'd been willing to trade the last gold coins you had for just a couple of them before you ran into me and Bob on that trail."

"You're right. They are valuable, and I don't want to abandon them either, but we've got to keep our options open. If it comes down to us or them, we'll do what we have to do. But we still don't need to be overburdened with stuff. I want to travel fast and light. It's the only way to do it, and I should be going alone, to tell you the truth. It would make a whole lot more sense. I can get there faster, and I can get past any dangers that may be out there better if I don't have to look out for the three of you."

"You know I can hold my own if trouble comes," Shauna said.

"You can. And Vicky did well too when she was put to the test."

"I can too, dude. You know I can man."

"When you're not crippled," Eric said. "As well-stocked as this place is, and secluded too, I wouldn't be worried at all about leaving the three of you here. It's just something to consider."

"But you know there's no way in hell I *will* consider it, don't you Eric Branson?"

"Yeah, Shauna. I know."

Jonathan could kind of see Eric's point, but Shauna wasn't having it, and if she and Vicky went, he sure wasn't going to stay here alone and wait. They might slow Eric down a little, but at least they would all get there together. Jonathan had already had all the alone time in the Colorado wilderness that he would ever need.

TEN

Eric felt like crap for leaving the way he did, but he knew he was doing what he had to do. He had made up his mind that it was in the best interest of everyone involved, whether they understood that or not. He didn't like the way he had to do it, and he knew that Shauna *damned sure* wasn't going to like it. Jonathan and Vicky would probably think he was an asshole too, but Eric couldn't help it. All of his professional life had been spent making strategic decisions, many of them difficult and painful to others, but he wasn't in the habit of second-guessing himself once those decisions had been made.

Eric came to his decision the afternoon after they'd buried Bob Barham near his cabin, but he'd been mulling over the idea since he'd first laid eyes on the place. Unlike the ranch belonging to Vicky's grandparents, Bob's place was truly off the grid and about as inaccessible as anywhere Eric could imagine in the Lower 48. Bob had done some hardcore planning and prepping to establish such an excellent hideaway and retreat, and especially to stock and equip it the way he had. Shauna, Jonathan and Vicky could spend a few weeks or even a few months there, if need be. If Eric hadn't thought it was safe, he wouldn't have considered leaving them there, but the truth was they would be better off there than with him and Eric would be safer too without them. Alone, he could travel hard, covering more distance and evading contact with others as much as possible. Jonathan especially, would be a liability to him with that broken leg, because if anything happened to the horses, the kid would be screwed. Shauna's hand was still far from a hundred percent too, even though she wasn't complaining, and after what Jonathan told him about the encounter on the bike trail, Eric knew he could count on her to persevere, pain or not. Still, it was better if she weren't put to the test like that again right now. Eric knew it was possible someone desperate would happen upon the cabin anyway, but if they did, he felt Shauna could handle it, especially with Jonathan and Vicky to back her up. Vicky had done surprisingly well in her face off with Gareth, not to mention the way she took those horses back from Brett. They were all survivors, but what he had to do now might call for a lot more than just that, and Eric would need all of his experience that could only be acquired in combat. There was simply no need to put them through that now that he had an alternative.

It wasn't just the well-stocked cabin that made his decision that afternoon either. Eric had also pored over Bob's topographical maps, looking at every possible option for getting to northern New Mexico from there. Along with the maps, Bob also had a collection of magazine and newspaper articles about the Continental Divide Trail, and from these Eric learned there was more to it than just the hiking trail. Using the existing network of forest service, BLM and other remote gravel roads, alternate routes and been mapped out for mountain bikers as well as off-road motorcyclists and four-wheel-drive enthusiasts. It seemed that the idea of traversing the country from Canada to Mexico along the spine of the continent was an appealing idea to many. Some parts of these routes were one and the same of course, but there were also places where they diverged more than a little, and these would give Eric some options. The main thing he gleaned from his study was that it *would* be possible to avoid well-traveled roads and most all pavement and still get where he needed to go. But to do this in any reasonable time frame was going to mean traveling hard and stopping little. Eric knew the kind of pushing he was capable of when there was no one to slow him down. The horses might suffer, but there was no reason for Shauna, Jonathan and Vicky to have to suffer too, other than the great disappointment that he knew they must be feeling about right now.

Disappointing Shauna was nothing new to Eric Branson though. He'd done it often enough throughout their marriage that it had ultimately resulted in divorce. Most of that he regretted, knowing he was to blame. This was different though, whether she would see it that way or not. Their ultimate objective in all of this, whether working together or separately, was to find Megan and get her to safety. Of course, Shauna wanted to be a part of it, and she had already, but she was going to have to sit this leg out, and he'd done his best to explain why in the letter he'd left for her before he slipped out into the night. He also warned her not to try and follow, no matter how much she might want to or how angry his leaving made her feel. He told her that she would never catch up and that the best thing she could do for Megan now was to be here for her when he brought her back, which he promised he would do, and soon. Eric didn't know if she'd torn the letter to shreds in a rage after reading it or not, but if he knew Shauna, he knew she would want to. She and Jonathan and Vicky were no doubt even now in a heated discussion about what to do, but he hoped that reason would prevail over emotion and they would come together to see his side of it.

Parting with Shauna so soon after finding her and Jonathan again wasn't easy for Eric either. This quest the two of them had embarked on had brought out something in her that Eric hadn't seen in a long time, and he had to admit that he liked it. His ability to do what had to be done now made him feel useful to her for the first time in so long. Now his life before made sense to her. He had skills and abilities to cope with a situation that overwhelmed lesser men. Shauna's world had turned upside down now, and suddenly *she* was in a war zone where men like Eric were at home. That other world where Daniel's money could provide her with security and stability was gone; at least for now, and Shauna had made her choice to leave him behind and go with Eric to find their daughter. It hadn't been Eric's intention to take her back from him, but he wondered now what would happen if they were together much longer and leaving now was one way to postpone having to find out. It had been so natural to kiss her that afternoon before and he hadn't wanted it to end then and he could tell that she didn't either. There was still something there between them, no matter how long it had been suppressed and put away, and it was hard not to think of the possibilities of a second chance, from an older and wiser perspective. The part of Eric that wanted to see if that could be wanted her with him on this journey. But the rational part kept him on track with his mission, reminding him that getting Megan came first, and that if he really cared about Shauna, it was best to leave her safely where she was.

Eric's careful inventory of the cabin had reassured him that the three of them wouldn't run out of any necessary supplies anytime soon. There was a huge stack of firewood ready to go and plenty more wood available to cut and split where that came from. Bob hadn't missed anything in his preparations, at least not anything significant that Eric could find. And while he loved his antique firearms and other frontier tools, he was also apparently wise enough to take advantage of modern technology as well. There was a Colt AR-15 in his gun collection, along with plenty of magazines and ammo for it; enough so that Eric felt good about taking as much as he needed for his own M4 while still leaving plenty behind with the rifle. With it and all of Bob's hunting rifles, shotguns and handguns, Shauna, Jonathan and Vicky were sufficiently armed to deal with any intruders, whether animal or human. They still had the rest of the horses too, if they needed them, but Eric had stressed in his letter that they'd be wise to stay close to the cabin and especially avoid the main trails.

Eric had only taken two horses and had chosen the mare named Maggie for his primary mount. She was the one that he'd first ridden that day he met Bob with Shauna on the trail, and since the two of them already knew each other, and he knew she had a good disposition, she was a good match for his limited riding experience. The packhorse Bob had brought with them that day was another mare named Sally, and Bob said she was easy to ride too. Eric had considered taking only Maggie and traveling much lighter but having the additional supplies the second animal could carry meant he wouldn't be distracted by looking for more along the way. And if something happened to Maggie, he would have a spare mount. Megan would need a ride for the trip back too, although Eric hoped she and Aaron would still have the horses they got from Vicky's grandfather. There was always the chance they would use some alternate transportation to return too, but there was no point in pondering that until the time came. If anything *could* begin to make Eric second-guess his decision, it was the thought of having to bring Megan all the way back to the cabin to get Shauna and the others before figuring out how to get back to Louisiana where *Dreamtime* was waiting.

Eric had barely slept the night before he left, tossing and turning instead as he waited for the hour to come. He'd managed to get all his stuff together unnoticed while going in and out for various chores the afternoon before. The saddlebags and packs were ready behind the woodshed, so that when he slipped out into the dark just before 0400, all he had to take was his rifle and sleeping bag. The cabin had a small upstairs loft that Vicky and Shauna were using, as the ladder going up there was impossible for Jonathan with the splint on his leg. Eric had thrown his own bag on the floor near the front door, which was hidden from view of the loft as it was directly overhead. All he had to do to get out unnoticed was to make sure Jonathan was still asleep, and from the kid's breathing patterns, it was easy to tell that he was.

Eric latched the door behind him and quickly saddled Maggie and loaded his packs onto Sally, leading them both as he started up the draw to the trail on foot. The ridge top route exposed him to bitter cold in the predawn hours, but now he was miles along and the midmorning sun warmed his face as he rode south.

When he passed the place where the gravel road led down and west to the ranch where he'd found Vicky, Eric gave it only a glance. He wondered for a moment about Brett and Jeremy, and whether they'd made the smart decision to leave the high country and go turn themselves in to a shelter or refugee camp. It wasn't an attractive proposition, Eric knew, but if they did it at least they wouldn't die of starvation. Eric had given them a chance by leaving them enough food to make the trek but if they didn't go it wasn't his problem. He had no time to make a side trip to the ranch to see, and he wasn't worried that they would find Bob's cabin because they had no idea even which way it was, and besides, he'd warned them they'd be shot on sight if he ever saw them again. From the looks on their faces after that last conversation, Eric didn't think either one of those two would push their luck.

As he continued on south, the only other thought Eric gave to Brett and Jeremy was the description they'd given him of the place where they'd last seen Colleen, the camp that Gareth had wanted to steal from, using her as bait. Eric was interested in investigating the site, not because he thought he could help her in any way at this point or that anyone would even be there, but simply because it wasn't far off the trail and he was curious. The boys had thought the men they saw there were members of some kind of militia group, and he figured any intel he could gather about that would be worth the effort. He'd already learned from the soldiers that drove him to the campus in Boulder that the army was focused on regaining control of the roads and populated areas and that the wilderness areas of the high country and other uninhabited or low population areas were a low priority for the foreseeable future. The only thing that would change that would be opportunities to strike specific targets, like the one Lieutenant Holton had sent him to investigate on that lakeshore back east.

It was expected that terrorist or insurgent groups would use remote areas as hideouts and bases of operation to plan further attacks, but only to a point. For them, being too removed from civilization would defeat their purpose because their targets were in the populated areas for the most part. But Eric didn't discount the possibility that other, possibly larger organizations were using such places to gather their forces. Some of the militia groups that anticipated something like this happening would be interested in completely restructuring things in the aftermath and controlling large areas of undisputed territory would be very much in their interest. If the gang that had detained Colleen and then tried to hunt down Jeremy and Brett were as well-equipped as the boys had said, then it was possible they were indeed part of something larger, or that they might be looking to join up with such a group. The last thing Eric wanted on his trek south was any contact with such an organization, but the best way to avoid them would be to know whether or not they really existed and where they were operating. Even if the bunch the boys had seen were the only ones out here, it was good to have a heads-up and know they were around in advance. Eric figured he'd be near the area of their camp in a couple more days of travel if the directions they'd given him were accurate.

"I doubt they'll be staying at that elevation much longer," Vicky had said when Eric was going over the location with her on Bob's maps in the cabin. "They'll freeze if they do."

"Well, if they *are* still there, that could be a good indication that they're not locals. Maybe they don't know any better. They may be tourists from Florida like us!"

Vicky had laughed at this, but she knew what the weather could be like here in the high country, and she strongly recommended that they pick the lower elevation alternatives for their route in every place that they had a choice. "Seriously guys, the weather up here is no joke. Trust me on this!"

Despite spending most of his formative years in south Florida though, Eric was no stranger to the cold. He'd operated in high mountain areas in places like Afghanistan and Pakistan, and more recently in parts of Europe. Dealing with winter weather was a real pain even without the complications it added to combat operations. It was another reason he wanted to move fast. He could beat the worst of the weather on the way south. Returning to the cabin might be another matter, but when he did that, he planned to have Megan with him, so it wouldn't matter if it took longer, waiting out storms or whatever was necessary.

When it was time to stop for the night, Eric turned off the trail in a low saddle where the slopes dropping down to the east side were heavily-timbered. It was too steep to ride comfortably at his level of experience, so Eric dismounted and led the horses until he was certain he was far enough down to be out of the wind and far enough off the trail that he and the horses wouldn't be seen or heard.

"My ears are burning, Maggie!" Eric said, gently rubbing the horse after taking off the saddle and laying it across a nearby log. "They're calling me every name in the book back at that cabin. Can you hear it too, girl? What about you Sally? Shauna is one unhappy woman, but I sure hope she does what I asked her to do, no matter how much she hates me for it!"

Eric tried not to think about the possibility that she wouldn't, and that she was so stubborn she had set out with Jonathan and Vicky anyway, determined to catch up to him. If Shauna had one trait that stood out above all others, it was hardheadedness! In many ways, it was a good thing. She made her decisions and stuck with them, come hell or high water, but trying that could get her and those kids hurt this time. If they left anyway and didn't catch up or find him, then what? He would have no way of knowing and might return weeks later with Megan only to have to start all over again, looking for them. He'd laid that argument out to her in his not-so-brief letter, but whether or not she'd let it sink through that thick skull of hers, was another matter. It sucked that he couldn't have just had a rational face-to-face conversation with all of them to tell them straight up what he planned to do but knew that wouldn't have worked; not with her, and especially not now, after she'd come this far. Eric knew he had to stop thinking about it and get some sleep, and he finally did, but something spooked the horses and woke him just a short time later.

Eric was on full alert within seconds, scanning the shadows around him in the forest with the night vision monocular, but finding nothing. He didn't know enough about traveling with horses in the wilderness to know what would or wouldn't make them jumpy. Had they caught a scent or heard something he couldn't hear? He was looking for something big and threatening, like a man, bear or mountain lion, but after a while, he concluded it could have been nothing at all, or maybe just some small nocturnal creature like a rabbit that the horses freaked out over anyway. Bob would know all their moods, but Eric would just have to guess and figure them out on his own as best he could. He whispered reassurance to them and then slid back into his sleeping bag inside the bivy, the M4 in reach close beside him and the custom blade his friend Drew had given him in its sheath inside the sleeping bag with him.

ELEVEN

THE NEXT DAY ERIC FOUND THE STREAM CROSSING where Brett and Jeremy claimed they'd lost all their supplies, and looking at the rapids below, he could see that it was a plausible scenario, especially for the inexperienced. He could hear the roar of a larger waterfall around the bend over the sound of the fast shoals in front of him. Eric didn't have to go have a look to know it was the one they told him about, over which their bags of stolen supplies had been swept out of reach and washed away. Seeing how easy such a thing could happen, with one simple misstep while fording, Eric wasn't taking any chances. He dismounted and led the horses upstream, working his way through dense thickets along the bank until he found a quieter place to cross. The last thing he wanted was to have to put down another horse for a broken leg, but both of the mares made it across without incident. He stopped on a sunny knoll to dry out and warm up, and by the second night's camp, he was beginning to feel better about leaving the way he did. Like he'd known he would, he'd made good time in those first two days, and he doubted he'd be near this far if they'd all come with him.

When morning came, he studied Bob's maps, comparing them to the actual landmarks he'd seen along his route as he worked out his plan for the day. He would reach the place he was seeking later today, and he studied the topography, working out the best and least-expected angle of approach in case the campsite was still occupied. The gravel road crossing that had led Gareth and his friends to leave the trail and find the camp was the most direct route, but Eric wasn't about to go walking down a wide-open road like that, where he might be seen from a distance. Like most of the places where roads crossed the trail, this one was in a pass, and parts of it were visible from above as he descended from a crest to the north. When he got there around mid-afternoon, Eric stopped and watched for several minutes, and then led the horses off the trail and secured them before setting out to make his approach.

He descended a steep wooded slope heading west, roughly parallel to the road, until he was several hundred feet lower and standing on the edge of a ravine overlooking a small stream. Jeremy and Brett had mentioned the stream, saying it crossed the road and ran behind the camp area, providing a handy water source. Eric wanted to approach from alongside the stream on the opposite bank. He could keep to thick cover that way and the noise of the fast-running water would mask any sound he might inadvertently make. Going that way meant that he would be close before he could see the site or even whether or not the tents were still there, but when he did get into position, he would be able to observe from much closer than the area out near the road from which the boys had seen it. They'd made several mistakes, which was to be expected given their youth, inexperience and lack of training in such matters. The worst of those mistakes was not watching long enough to really determine who they were dealing with and how many there were. But Eric didn't like surprises, and patience was something he didn't have a problem with when it came to situations like this.

His circuitous route took him a full hour, but he was glad he'd made the choice when he finally got a look through the trees and saw tents still there. At least one of them was occupied, as he could see through the open flaps enough to make out the boots and lower legs of at least two men, probably sitting at a table inside eating or playing cards. He didn't see anyone else at first glance, but grazing nearby, in a makeshift barbed-wire corral, were several horses, more than half of them bearing similar spotted patterns as the Appaloosa gelding that Vicky had been riding when she had her final confrontation with Gareth. Eric knew when he saw them that these horses were also from the ranch, and their presence was proof enough for him that these were indeed the men who'd raided and burned the place before killing Vicky's grandparents.

Eric was sure too that the occupants of this camp were also responsible for Colleen's disappearance. The tents were as the boys described them; old-fashioned looking canvas wall tents with big wooden poles and stove pipes passing through their roofs. They were the kind of expedition tents that were common back in the day before lightweight nylon coverings and aluminum frames came into existence, and were still favored by hunting outfitters and others setting up base camps in cold-weather conditions. They certainly weren't the kinds of tents you carried in a backpack, but Eric saw several big quad ATVs with cargo racks parked nearby. There were stacks of boxes and crates around the perimeter, many of them bearing markings that identified them as military property, no doubt stolen from a National Guard depot or convoy. Most of this stuff was covered with canvas tarps, but out in the open there were propane tanks and large metal gas cans, the latter no doubt containing fuel for the ATVs. The absence of trucks or other full-sized vehicles was likely due to the condition of the 'road,' which was really just a two-track trail, too rough and narrow for most anything but ATVs.

Whatever it was these people were up to, Eric knew at a glance it was pretty well organized and serious. This wasn't just a bunch of hunters who'd decided to bug out up here until things calmed down. The camp was arranged with military precision and efficiency, with everything sorted and in its place, right down to the parking of the ATVs. Eric still didn't see a guard posted on site, but a few more minutes of watching revealed movement out among the trees a couple of hundred yards to the east, exactly in the area that he would have crossed had he approached from the road the way Gareth and his buddies had. Eric watched until two men materialized, dressed in camo BDUs and carrying M4-type rifles. They weren't heading back to the tents, but instead were working their way around, likely on a scheduled patrol of the perimeter. How many others might be around or occupying the tents, Eric couldn't tell. It was either watch and wait until dark to find out, or speed things up by questioning these two fellows he could see. Eric was patient, but he also had a long journey ahead of him and didn't want to spend a lot of time here if he could get the information he sought sooner, so he chose the second option. They would tell him whether or not Colleen was there too, Eric was quite sure of it.

That the two were walking together and appeared to be in conversation told Eric that they probably weren't really expecting a threat at the moment. It was a logical assumption, considering the location, and he figured they may not have had visitors here since the day Gareth and his friends showed up. But the fact that there was a patrol at all told him that there was some semblance of military discipline and experience here, which backed up his previous presumption that this wasn't just a bunch of hunting buddies. Eric watched the two as they headed north across the rutted two-track road. If they were going to circle around the camp from there, they would soon cross the creek he'd followed to get to where he was presently watching, and Eric figured they would wind their way around in a big circle through the more open woods on the rise behind him. The place to intercept them would be down in the thickets near the streamside, and Eric decided to move closer to where he anticipated they would cross and then come up behind them once they were on the other side. It didn't bother him that there was two of them, despite the fact that it might be a little harder to gain control without alerting the others in the tents. Eric only needed one of them in a condition to talk in order to get his answers, and whatever he did to his partner might be convincing motivation for the survivor to loosen his tongue.

With his decision made, Eric moved out, slipping silently down the stream bank until he caught a glimpse of the two again just as they were crossing, using large rocks as stepping stones to avoid getting their feet wet. Eric could hear enough to tell that they were indeed talking now, but their voices were muted by the gurgle of running water so that he couldn't make out any of it. It didn't matter anyway, other than to prove to him that they were in fact, overly complacent and unaware. He watched them work their way into the thicket as they climbed out of the creek bottom, and then he moved in to follow. The time to take them was now, while they were in the heaviest cover well out of sight of the tents and far enough that any noises other than gunshots probably wouldn't be heard. Eric drew his knife as he stalked them from behind. The thicket naturally forced them into single file as they pushed through it, but the low chatter of their conversation continued, nevertheless. Eric closed in on the one in the rear, the one unfortunate enough to be his first target simply because of position. That one Eric had to silence quickly and permanently. The man was completely unaware he had just seconds to live, of course, as he blabbed on to his companion, just three or four steps ahead.

Eric rushed him, grabbing hold of his face from behind with his left hand just a split second before plunging his six-inch blade downward at an angle into the side of his neck, just behind the clavicle. A muffled cry and the rustle of leaves as the man began to struggle caused his companion to stop and turn around, and Eric shoved the one he'd stabbed into the other as hard as he could, knocking him off balance before he could raise his rifle. Eric was on him in another second. The knife was still embedded in the first one, but he didn't need it as he took the second guy down with his weight as he dove into him, slamming him hard enough onto the rocky ground to take away his breath. Eric drove a solid punch into the man's nose for good measure, then drew his Glock and shoved it into his temple. The fear in the man's eyes told Eric that he understood the gravity of his situation, but Eric wanted to be sure.

"Stay perfectly still or I'll put a round through your skull right now!" Eric said, as he glanced back at the other man, not quite dead yet, but assuredly no longer a threat. "Do you understand?"

The man beneath him nodded. Eric studied his face, now bloodied from his busted nose and figured him to be in his late twenties or maybe early thirties. His haircut was military short, and he was lean and fit, as if still actively training for combat. Eric figured he'd likely served before, and that it was why he'd gravitated to an outfit such as this, whatever it was. "You're a veteran right? What were you Army? Marines? What?" Eric asked, pushing the Glock harder against his skull."

"Army. Not anymore! Screw that bullshit!"

"So, what are you and your buddies up to out here?"

"Nothing! What does it look like? We're just surviving, that's all. But I guess that's illegal now, huh? Is that why they sent you? Where is the rest of your unit?"

"No one sent me," Eric said, lifting himself off the man and pulling him up to a sitting position before shoving him back hard against the trunk of a sapling pine. Eric then pulled his hands behind the tree and using one of the large zip-ties he'd found among Bob's supplies, secured his wrists. "I came alone, and I came to get answers. You're going to provide them, or you'll bleed out here like your friend," Eric nodded at the nearby body. "Now, start with your name:"

"It's Matthews," the man said.

"So, you did your time in the Army, but now you're

out. "Was it Private Matthews?"

The man nodded.

"So, who are you with now, Private Matthews? The insurrectionists?"

"Like hell! Screw those commie bastards!"

"Oh, I got it! So, you're not trying to help *them* fight the government, yet I see that you have stolen government property stashed down there by those tents. And stolen weapons!" Eric picked up both of the rifles the two had been carrying. "Military-issue M4s—the real deal— and your buddy's even has the grenade launcher! You didn't buy this stuff at the local gun show, did you, Private Matthews? So, what are you and your fellow former-soldier buddies getting ready for? Is it a militia organization you're a part of? Are you guys just waiting it out until you see who wins so you can decide whose side you're on? Or do you plan on taking on the winners too and doing your own thing? Let me guess; there's a lot more of you than just the handful of fanatics in this camp, right?"

"You're damned right there's more. More than you could ever imagine! You're making a big mistake if you think you can interfere with our business too. I don't care who you're with!"

"I could care less about your cause, one way or the other," Eric said. "But I am interested in this particular unit at this camp, which includes you, Private Matthews, because I'm looking for a girl that disappeared here; a college-aged redhead named Colleen. I know she walked right into this place asking for help, and I know that she didn't leave. I also know that her male companions barely escaped the men that tried to hunt them down. And I know that the girl must have been forced to talk, because shortly afterwards armed men showed up at the ranch where she and her friends had been staying. Those men killed the innocent old man and woman that owned the place and burned down their house after first taking all their stuff, including the rest of the horses."

"We don't do stuff like that..."

Eric smacked him before he could finish his sentence. "Shut up! I'm not finished! Those Appaloosa horses I just saw near the tents match the description of the ones missing from that ranch. I'm not interested in hearing your bullshit! I'm here because I want to know if the girl is still alive, and if so, where she is. If you don't want to tell me, then after I kill you, I'll go and kill the rest of your crew one by one until I get the answers I came for. Is that understood, Matthews? *Now, where is she?*"

"I don't know man! But she's not here!"

"But she *was* here, right? Is that what you're trying to tell me, Matthews?" Eric backhanded the other side of his face hard enough to slam his head against the rough bark of the tree he was bound to.

"Maybe. I don't know! Look man, there have been a lot of people through here we that detained. I don't remember them all!"

"It wasn't that long ago!" Eric said. "You wouldn't

forget a pretty redhead, would you, Matthews?" Eric grabbed him by the throat and squeezed, bringing his face close to his, his eyes boring into the other's with an intensity he couldn't squirm away from. "Where is she now, Matthews?"

"Okay! Yeah, I think she *was* here, but not for long!"

"Why not? Where is she then, if she's not still here?"

"I don't know man!"

"Then you're of no more use to me then." Eric said, as he released his grip and got up slowly, making sure the man was watching as he turned and bent to withdraw his knife, still buried to the hilt at the junction of the dead man's neck and shoulder. When he turned back to Matthews with the bloody blade in hand, he found him suddenly more talkative.

"I guess they took her where they've been taking all of them. That's all I know!"

"Who's 'they' and where is this place they're taking all of 'who' to?" Eric asked.

"Some of our people. They come to resupply us and to take any prisoners we've picked up in the area. We're assigned to this sector to watch the roads and trails here, especially that hiking trail, because it's had a lot of traffic ever since we've been here."

"So, you're out here to capture people using the trail? By whose authority and why?"

"Just the commie college punks, man! They're the ones that started most of this shit, rioting and burning down buildings. We've caught some of them using the trails and backroads, probably so they can join up with more of their kind and start more shit. They backpack through the mountains to avoid the police and soldiers on the roads."

"What does that have to do with you though? Why are you trying to stop them?"

"Because this is our country, man! The government won't do anything about it. They're just as much to blame as anybody. They might be in control of the roads and the cities, but they can't do shit up here. They're spread too thin as it is already dealing with all that crap down there. We're in control of these mountains and we aim to keep outsiders out. Let 'em all kill each other fighting over their shithole cities. That's all right with us, because when it's all over, *we'll* be the ones to mop it up!"

Eric laughed. "You and how many of your buddies in your little private army? You do realize that the U.S. military is expanding its reach everywhere right? All the major interstates and highways are full of command posts and checkpoints. This situation will be brought under control, however long it takes."

"So what? They won't be able to control *us* by blocking roads. And there's more of us than you think. We will...."

Eric brought the bloody knife back up to the man's throat before he could go on. "Let's cut to the chase, Matthews!" he said, applying slight pressure with the edge to let him know he would finish the job if he didn't comply. "There's another girl I'm looking for too. In fact, she's the real reason I'm here, and I know that she was using that trail too, heading south on horseback, maybe two weeks ago. She's a brunette, 20 years old, and would have been ahead of the redhead and her friends, maybe by a couple of days, and she was traveling with a young man who looks full-blooded Native American. They were both college students too, and I want to know if they were among these 'prisoners' you took from the trail, and where they are now."

"I haven't seen anybody like that, man. I doubt they came through here, because if they would have, we would have seen them. But we've got people watching all the trails and roads anywhere near the divide. If they're outsiders and they tried to get through these mountains on horseback, you can bet your ass they didn't make it. They're either dead or in the prison camp with the others, and you will be too if you don't turn around and go back to wherever it is you came from."

Eric only needed a few more pieces of information from this man. First, he had to be sure there was no one being held there inside the tents now. Secondly, he needed the location of this other, so-called 'prison camp' to which all those caught 'trespassing' had been taken. Almost all of the land in these mountains through which the divide trail passed was open to the public, as it was government owned, rather than private; most of it admin- istered by the National Forest Service or Bureau of Land Management. Eric knew this from studying the maps of the route in Bob's cabin, and of course, he knew much of the mountain country of the American west fit that description even before he had reason to study those particular maps. His other questions were in regard to more details of the larger organization this man was a part of. If what he told him was true, it was more extensive than Eric would have guessed, but then Lieutenant Holton and some of the other military personnel he'd come into contact with on his way out here had mentioned the possibility. The build-up to this situation had been going on for so many years that there was plenty of time for serious organization and numbers building on both sides. In truth, it was a low-intensity war that was unfolding here, and like it or not Eric was involved in it just as much as he'd been involved in all the other wars in which he'd fought around the globe. The face of the enemy was different, and perhaps harder to identify, but he knew for sure that he was looking at one now, and for what these men had already done, Eric could afford them no mercy. He couldn't take a chance that this one would sound a warning that he was here or that any survivors left behind would come after him. He made it quick when he dispatched Matthews and then wiped and put away his blade before rolling the other dead man over to retrieve several M203 grenades and the extra rifle mags he had on him. The grenades especially, would come in handy for what he had to do next. The indiscriminate hostage-taking of refugees on a public trail was about to come to an end, at least here.

TWELVE

IT WAS ALMOST TOO EASY IT WENT SO SMOOTH. Regardless of whatever prior combat experience some of these men might have had, they clearly weren't expecting anyone to bring the fight to them up here. Until now, they'd been the top predators here, ambushing travelers with the element of surprise and their greater numbers and superior weapons, but none of that helped them now. Eric had caught them totally off-guard in the middle of the afternoon, completely relying on the two he'd already taken out to keep watch and alert them to danger, which they weren't expecting anyway. But those two had become complacent because of the quiet here, walking together and talking when they should have been on opposites sides of the perimeter as they made their rounds. Now Eric had the information he wanted as well as the weapons two dead men would never need again. He used the latter to unleash hell on the rest of their companions, killing them all before they even knew what hit them.

The first M203 anti-personnel round exploded just inside the open door of the tent he already knew was occupied. Eric followed up with another that landed in front of another tent before dumping a mag on burst mode into the first tent. When the few that survived the initial onslaught began emerging from the other tents, trying to figure out what was going on, Eric cut them down with more rifle fire. It was over in minutes, but he waited and watched for several more, just to make sure, before moving in to be sure the job was finished, searching from tent to tent for survivors, and finishing off the wounded that he found. Eric then looked for anything that might indicate that the girls or Aaron had been there, but finding nothing, he opened the gate to let the horses loose and then went and retrieved Maggie and Sally, bringing them back so he could stash the extra rifles and more M203 rounds into his packs and saddle-bags. There was a lot of good stuff there among the stolen supplies, but Eric couldn't carry anymore, nor did he really need it. He emptied the gasoline cans on the sides of the tents and over the ATVs and wooden crates, and then set fire to all of it and rode away.

Eric knew now that his encounter with Jeremy and Brett was fortunate, even though it resulted in the death of Bob Barham. If they had not come back to the ranch when they did, then chances were he and Shauna and Jonathan and Bob would have ridden unaware into this militia-occupied territory, which would have been bad enough. But worse, he wouldn't know about the taking of hostages that was going on, and the very good possibility that Megan and Aaron had fallen into the hands of some of those guys just as Colleen had. But now he was armed with knowledge, and Eric was going to make use of it. He had to keep moving at the moment to put distance between himself and that burning camp, but going forward, he would take even greater precautions than normal. The threat now was not just the possibility of running into random gangs of desperados like some of those he'd encountered down south. Now he was in the midst of a much larger and far more organized resistance movement, at least if that Matthew's fellow was to be believed. As a result, Eric was going to have to alter his route, especially when it came to the divide trail, which might lead him into an ambush.

But regardless of that, he was still going to be moving in the same general direction. Matthews had told him that the larger militia camp where the prisoners were being held was to the south, and so Eric would not be going much out of his way to visit it in order to determine whether or not Megan and Aaron were there before continuing on to the reservation in New Mexico if they weren't. As far as Colleen's predicament, Eric would make that decision after finding the place and making his assessment. If there was something he could do, he would, but not at the cost of compromising his ultimate mission of finding Megan. Colleen and her boyfriend

Brett made a big mistake when they left with Gareth on those stolen horses, but Eric figured she probably had no idea what she was getting into. That was the problem with all these kids, even his own daughter. Eric could only hope that some of the things he'd taught Megan early on had sunk in and would come back to her now that she might need them.

He stopped before it got too dark to study the maps, so he could plan the next stage of his route. The militia camp he was looking for was accessible from a gravel forest service road that dead-ended at the edge of a designated roadless wilderness area. Going the most direct way, along the trail to where that particular road crossed, it was about 20 miles away. The two-track dirt road behind the camp he just left connected to another little-used logging road that also intersected the one he sought. That was the route the militia used to transport goods and move the prisoners on their ATVs, so Eric knew there was a good chance he'd run into someone if he went that way. Another option he saw on the map was a steep hiking trail that turned off the main divide trail and crossed over a pass about five miles to the north of the valley where the road dead-ended at the camp. Eric figured he could go that way, walking and leading the horses if it was too steep to ride, and then work his way down to the camp by bushwhacking cross-country. It would be slower going, but the best bet to avoid running into one of their patrols. He knew from what Matthews told him that this encampment was one of the militia's main outposts in the region, and that there were at least 50 or 60 armed men there, maybe a lot more. If he were to have any hope of finding out if Megan was being held there, he had to approach with great stealth, giving them no reason to be on heightened alert. The only thing that might blow that plan, Eric knew, was if someone from there went back and found the other camp that he'd just wiped out. That gave him reason enough to push himself to exhaustion getting there, as the longer route would nearly double the miles he had to travel. The moon was going to be nearly full tonight though, so nighttime travel was feasible, even though the temperatures after dark would be frigid. The chances of running into a patrol at night would be slim, but he still had his night vision monocular with which to scan any open areas he had to cross before leaving cover.

Eric reached the side trail he was looking for at around at 1100 hours. As he'd deduced from the map, it was much smaller and steeper than the main divide trail, which was almost a road in comparison. Walking it was the only sensible thing to do, especially in the dark, but Eric didn't mind. He was already saddle-sore from being unaccustomed to riding, but he could out-walk most people in any kind of terrain, and having the horses meant he didn't have to carry anything on his back. He walked fast when he was moving, as it kept him warmer, but he still took the precaution of stopping at regular intervals to look and listen.

Before daylight came, he'd crossed the road he'd seen

on the map and was winding his way up a switchback route to the pass north of his destination. He found a hidden spot among the rocks halfway up to rest for two or three hours in the midmorning sun, and then pressed on, determined to locate the militia camp before nightfall, and then approach closer under the cover of darkness. Eric figured the nearer he got to the camp, the more likely it was that there could be security patrols or other activity out beyond the perimeter. With that in mind, he decided to leave the horses on the north side of the pass, unburdened and hobbled the way Shauna had shown him so that they could graze freely but not wander off too far. With the saddle and his other gear stashed among the rocks, Eric set off on foot to crest the pass and begin the long descent down the other side. The trail there followed a dry stream bed until he had dropped another thousand feet to the first of several live springs. He knew the camp was supposed to be near this same stream, another couple thousand feet lower where it was much bigger. The road ended there where the wilderness boundary line began.

Eric was sure that the road would be barricaded and guarded, probably a good distance out from the camp itself. Whether they would take the precaution of posting guards along the creek, both upstream and down, he didn't know, but from that point forward he moved with much more caution. It was too risky to simply follow the trail that roughly paralleled the creek, so instead, Eric stayed on the western ridge above it, picking his way down while keeping in the cover of the trees and other vegetation as much as possible. That last few miles took him all afternoon as a result, but he was certain he'd not been seen as he finally reached a rock outcrop from which he could see the meadow at the end of the road. Eric scanned the grassy, open area with his binoculars, expecting to see more tents, vehicles and armed men, but there was nothing manmade or moving in sight, and he wondered if he'd come to the wrong place. He knew the Matthews guy could have been lying to him, although he felt he was getting the truth as the man knew he had nothing left to lose. Eric continued to search with the glasses, and even though he saw nothing, the one thing he noticed was that it was quiet; except for the noisy racket of crows somewhere in the distance. Something was off about this place, but until he investigated further, he wouldn't know what it was.

Eric made his way downhill until he reached the creek and hopping across in several big steps onto exposed boulders, he crossed it and then started up the other side to try and get a view of the road. As he topped the crest of the small ridge on that side, the smell of death reached his nostrils just before he noticed the flocks of crows clustered in the tall pines below. Hundreds more of them were on the ground across the road, which he could see now, and when Eric brought the binoculars into focus on the scene before him, he suddenly understood why they were there. Bodies were scattered everywhere among the rocks, twisted and contorted, some whole and others not so much. Farther back among the trees, Eric could now see bullet-riddled and burned-out pickup trucks as well as ATVs like the ones at the other camp, along with the blackened rubble of several structures. He studied the scene long enough to convince himself that nothing living but the scavengers was among them, and then Eric made his way down to the road.

He'd found the right place all right, but not before someone else did. Eric walked past the first of the dead he came to, all of them men that he assumed had been members of the militia. Whoever had killed them had picked up their weapons and magazines but had left the bodies to rot where they fell. They'd been like that a few days, Eric was sure, but not long enough that the birds and coyotes were done mopping up. As he moved among them, the noisy crows eyed him from a safe distance, resenting him for disturbing their grisly feast. Eric's heart was racing as he moved towards the middle of what had been the camp. Had the prisoners being held here met the same fate as their guards? Eric didn't know but judging from what he could piece together of it, a larger force had attacked the camp from the ground. There was nothing like flattened trees to indicate that an airstrike or heavy ordinance had been used, but grenades and other portable explosives might have come into play, judging by the blown off limbs and missing heads of some of the bodies. He found various metal objects that survived the fires that had destroyed the tents and supplies, but the attackers had been thorough in picking up any weapons or ammunition that may still be usable. From the looks of it, Eric was beginning to think it was a military operation. He couldn't imagine another insurgent group strong enough to attack this one with both the overwhelming force and precision needed to pull this off.

He found what he was looking for near the far end of the encampment; a large, pavilion-sized area with blackened metal poles still standing, the canvas coverings making up the roof and walls burned away. Razor wire fencing surrounded the whole thing, except for one side that had been pulled away. Eric knew this was likely an enclosure to house prisoners, and he steeled himself for what he might find as he stepped past the wire to examine several blackened bodies he saw inside. If Megan was among them, his journey would end then and there. It was a hard thing to think about, but Eric knew all too well the reality of conflict and that collateral damage was to be expected even if whoever attacked this place wasn't out to kill everyone present. But though there was one female among the dead, she definitely wasn't Megan and from what he could tell, she didn't fit Colleen's description either. Eric walked out of the enclosure feeling a huge sense of relief that he didn't find his worst nightmare. After sweeping the rest of the entire camp area, checking each and every one of the bodies, he found none that he thought could be Megan's friend Aaron either.

It was growing dark by the time Eric was finished, and he was anxious to leave that place and return to where he'd left his horses. On the way back, he had a lot of time to think about what he'd seen. His best estimate based on the state of the bodies he'd found was that the attack had probably taken place at least three days prior and maybe up to a week. Whoever had done it was long gone and apparently had no interest in occupying the area afterward, giving Eric more reason to believe it was a military operation targeting that particular group. It was surprising though, considering the location. From what he'd gathered from the soldiers he'd traveled with earlier; the mountain areas were mostly off their radar. Eric figured the only explanation was that this group had initiated some extreme action that drew their interest enough to merit such a coordinated operation. Whoever they were, they'd been thorough and had certainly gotten the job done.

Eric knew that just because he didn't find Megan, Colleen or Aaron among the dead didn't mean they hadn't been there though. While the bodies he did find in the enclosure were no doubt some of the prisoners, that didn't mean that there weren't others that were rescued or taken into custody by the attackers. But if that were the case, then how would he ever find out, much less find them? The other possibility, of course, was that Megan and Aaron had somehow eluded the militia members and made their way through the mountains without being captured. If so, Eric figured they may be closing in on the reservation in New Mexico soon, if they weren't already there, so he had a decision to make.

Would it be worth his time to go back looking for clues as to where the attacking force came from and where they went afterward? Or should he continue on as he originally planned, and ride to the one place that he knew was Megan's planned destination?

Eric slept a few hours after returning to his horses, and the next morning he was hiking back down to the site of the attack, leading Maggie and Sally down the narrow trail. He had no need to walk amongst the dead again to look for more clues in what had been the camp, but he did circle wider beyond the perimeter, and as he expected, he found plenty of shell casings back within the trees inside of easy rifle range, most of them 5.56. He found enough to know that the assault had come from two directions, catching the occupants of the camp in a crossfire, and knowing what he did about such operations, Eric figured there'd been more men stationed somewhere along the road to the east to prevent any survivors from escaping in that direction. He could tell that vehicles had been using the road too, but whether the tracks were made by the militia members or the assault team, he couldn't be sure. He continued to proceed carefully along the road to the east, leading the horses, as he had to go that way anyway to intersect the Divide Trail again in order to continue heading south.

The one thing that bothered him about going on to New Mexico though was the fact that he'd found no sign of Colleen. He still believed that the Matthews guy was telling the truth when he said she was being taken there though. There was no reason to think he'd made it up, especially since he'd found the camp exactly where he said it would be. *So, if Colleen wasn't among the dead, then where was she? Did her absence mean that the soldiers had rescued her and perhaps some of the other people being held there as well?* That possibility meant Megan and Aaron could be among them, and it presented Eric with no small amount of doubt, but when he reached the trail, he still decided to go on the theory that Megan had never been captured in the first place. Otherwise, he would lose no telling how much time trying to locate the nearest military post and when he did, it was unlikely that he would be given the information he sought. In fact, it was much more likely that he would be mistaken for one of those militia types himself and shot at on sight. At the very least, he would be disarmed and detained if he approached any such place, creating yet another delay to add to the countless others he'd endured already. Eric decided he didn't need that. He would trust his instincts and go to the reservation first, and if Megan *wasn't* there, then he'd consider his other options.

THIRTEEN

MEGAN BRANSON KNEW SHE WAS TAKING A BIG chance by making contact with the soldiers, but she didn't know what else to do. There was nothing she could do for Aaron without help, and she didn't think she could possibly reach his own people before it was too late. And even if she did make it there, she wasn't sure they would believe her, if they were even willing to talk to her at all. Aaron had said he was quite sure the reservation would be off-limits to outsiders by now, which was part of the reason he was taking her there. As long as the tribe stayed on their own lands and didn't get involved in the affairs of the federal government and the groups fighting against it and each other, he felt sure they would be left alone. The reservation would be a safe refuge for them both, and Aaron assured her she would be welcomed as long as she was with him. But how could they have known what they would encounter along the route? Megan had never been under any delusions that the journey south through the mountains would be easy, much less completely safe, but with Aaron's knowledge of the wilderness, she'd felt their chances of getting through were good. She'd already seen his competence as a hunter and woodsman on the trek from Boulder, and then during their stay at the ranch. She trusted they would both survive because of his abilities, but now she was alone and no one but her knew or cared about his plight. Megan was determined not to let him down, even if it meant putting herself at great risk.

As long as Aaron was being held against his will, Megan couldn't even think about her ultimate goal of getting home to Florida. Even if she wanted to try, she knew soldiers like these would stop her. They didn't care that she was 2000 miles away from home or if she ever made it back or not. Their task was to secure the road-ways wherever they were posted, and the rumors were that was in strategic locations along all the major high-ways in the country. Megan was approaching this check-point from the wilderness though, working her way down a steep trail winding out of a roadless area where the authorities were absent for now. She hoped they would take an interest in the information she had to give them, but she knew it was a gamble whether or not they would hear her out. In order to have a chance of talking before she was arrested, she knew she had to approach in a non-threatening manner. That meant going unarmed; something she was loath to do these days, but she kept

telling herself that what she was doing, she was doing for
Aaron. He had already risked everything to help her, and
now he was paying for it. Doing the same for him was the
least she could do.

Megan paused to study the scene on the roadway
below as she gathered the courage to go forward. The
roadblock on this two-lane highway consisted of two
large military supply trucks parked perpendicular across
it, bumper to bumper, as well as three of the rugged off-
road vehicles Megan knew were Humvees. A small
portable building set up nearby undoubtedly served as a
base for the men stationed there, and Megan doubted the
vehicles were moved much, if ever. The purpose was to
prevent unauthorized traffic flow, and if what she'd heard
was true, the reasoning was that this would disrupt
terrorist and insurrectionist activity by limiting their
mobility. Of course, it also resulted in shutting down the
economy and interfering with all the activities of innocent civilians at the same time, and it was why she and
her friends had come all this way from Boulder using
trails through the mountains. Now, she had to come out
in the open to face the very thing she'd gone to such
effort to avoid, and it would either work out in the end or
it would not.

The only weapon she had on her was the .45 auto-
matic pistol that Vicky's grandfather had given her when
she and Aaron told him of their plans to head to New
Mexico. Megan had felt bad about taking it, but the kind
old man had said he had lots of guns and ammo, and that

this particular pistol was one he wouldn't miss. He'd given Aaron a .30-30 hunting rifle as well, and both of them enough ammo to see them through. Having the pistol made Megan feel better, especially now that she was alone, but it had done her no good when Aaron was taken. Armed or not, the odds weren't in her favor to intervene, and Megan had done the only thing she could do at the time. She had saved herself so that she could escape and figure out a way to save Aaron.

She unfastened her belt and removed the holstered pistol, hiding it in a crevice of rock near a tall lightning-struck and splintered spruce that she hoped she'd be able to easily locate again if and when she returned. Then, she stood and resolutely began walking down the trail, no longer attempting to stay out of sight of the soldiers. When she reached an open area at the turn of another switchback, Megan stopped and waved her hands over-head, shouting at the men below as she did. The soldiers weren't expecting an approach from that angle, and for a second, she was frozen in fear as she saw them scramble to move behind their vehicles and saw a swivel-mounted machine gun atop one of the Humvees swing around in her direction. Megan kept her hands high over her head, afraid to move and totally at the mercy of the men behind those guns until they decided what to do. Then she heard a voice address her from a loudspeaker from one of the vehicles:

"DO NOT MOVE! KEEP YOUR HANDS OVER YOUR HEAD AND STAY WHERE YOU ARE!"

Megan did exactly as she was told, watching and waiting as four men with rifles started up the slope in her direction, all of them scanning the rocks and vegetation surrounding her, no doubt wary of an ambush.

"I'm alone!" Megan yelled to them, as they drew near, all of them covering her with their weapons.

When the soldiers closed in, two of them kept their distance, still looking for signs of accomplices, while the other two moved near to either side, ordering her to drop to her knees at gunpoint and then to put her hands behind her back. Megan felt her wrists squeezed together as a plastic zip tie was locked into place around them, and then the two men pulled her to her feet, one on each side gripping her upper arms.

"This is a restricted area with no trespassing allowed," one of the men said. "You're lucky you weren't shot on sight!"

"I didn't know that, sir," Megan said. "I've been in the backcountry on the trails. I haven't been anywhere near any of the restricted highways and roads in weeks. But I came this way looking for help. That's why I waved to you guys."

"You're under arrest now, young lady. I don't want to hear your story. You can tell it to my sergeant before we call in for transport to have you processed into the system. Let's go!"

Megan knew better than to argue and she had no choice but to follow orders as the soldier prodded her from behind with his rifle barrel in the small of her back.

She was scared now, wondering if she'd made a terrible mistake, but she already knew from the tone in this man's voice and the demeanor of his three companions, that further questions now would get her nowhere. Her best bet was with this sergeant he spoke of, so she focused her attention now on getting down the steep rocky trail without falling, a task in itself with her hands tied behind her.

All eyes were upon her as the rest of the men manning the blockade stood waiting on the four to lead her down to where the vehicles were parked across the pavement. Megan knew that if she was going to get anywhere with these men, she was going to have to go along with their protocol and show them respect, whether she wanted to or not. Her dad had taught her enough that she knew what the game was all about, and they had literally made a game of it back in the days when she actually got to spend some time with him. Those were the years before her parents' divorce, when her dad would be there sometimes for a few weeks between missions. She remembered going to the range with him and becoming proficient at shooting at an age when the other girls she went to school with had never even handled a firearm. Her dad had taught her many useful things when he was around, but she resented the fact that he always left again, usually for months, if not years. She had no idea where he was right now, or whether he was alive or dead, but if the fact that he was a former Navy SEAL could give her some leverage with these Army dudes, Megan was going to use it. She got her chance when she was taken before the sergeant in command of the roadblock.

Megan gave the man her full name, date of birth and home address. Then she explained that she was a student at the university in Boulder and that she'd left there to escape the riots and violence that had taken over the campus and the city.

"Why did you go into the mountains, if you weren't mixed up with the troublemakers? There were shelters in place for students that needed a place to go."

"We left because my roommate's grandfather had a ranch way out in the mountains. We thought it would be safe to go there, but then we got separated and it was just me and my friend, Aaron. I was going with him to his family's place in New Mexico when this happened." Megan left out the details about going to the ranch and then leaving because of Gareth. She was focused instead on the immediate problem; the fact that she and Aaron had inadvertently wandered into an area taken over by a heavily-armed militia group, and that Aaron had been taken captive while protecting her. "I'm just looking for help, sir," she said. "I knew the Army would be interested in knowing about those militia guys and where they are, so I came looking for the first outpost I could find. I figured you would be grateful to get first-hand intel from on the ground."

The sergeant gave her a funny look at this statement. "Intel from on the ground, huh?"

"My dad told me a lot of stories about the missions he did. A big part of his job was observation behind enemy lines, setting up airstrikes and things like that. He said it was critical to get the details right, and I did. I know exactly where this place is."

"Behind enemy lines, huh? So, your dad was in the service?"

"Yes, sir! The Navy. He was a SEAL team operator and he did all kinds of dangerous missions behind enemy lines."

The sergeant was skeptical until Megan persisted, giving him some of the details Eric had told her until he no longer doubted that her father had indeed served. But that didn't convince him that she had any worthwhile information as she claimed.

"I'm telling you, I saw it firsthand. This is not some little gang of looters hiding out up there. They're gathering forces in those mountains, and they're getting ready to do something big. I don't know what that might be, but I know that there's a lot of them and that they have all kinds of equipment. The kind of stuff they couldn't have just bought before all this started."

The more she told him, the more Megan could tell that she had the sergeant's interest. Now they were sitting inside his field office in the portable building, and he'd said enough to indicate that the presence of this militia group in the nearby mountains was known to them and doing something about it was already on the agenda. That was one reason for the location of this particular checkpoint, as the road they were on was one of the few access points to the area. Megan's timing in coming here with this information was good, so she was careful to give him as many details as she could remember, starting from the beginning:

"Aaron and I did our best to never get separated while we were on the trail," Megan said, "but that afternoon we'd found the perfect place to camp under a rock overhang just far enough off the trail to be out of sight. The only problem was that the closest water was a little creek we could barely make out through the trees, about a quarter mile farther down the trail and several hundred feet lower. Aaron said there was no point in us both going, because I could start gathering wood for a fire. So, he left the saddles with me and went by himself to water the horses. I didn't think much about it, because we hadn't seen anybody in two days, but about fifteen minutes later, I heard shouting.

"It was more than one voice and none of them sounded like Aaron. I couldn't see anything from where I was, so I started down there to see what was going on, but I didn't want anyone to see me until I knew who was there. Aaron had the rifle with him, so I wasn't really worried, but I grabbed the pistol we had too, just in case. We had been very careful to avoid other people as much as possible, and we never expected to have to use them, but we always kept the guns loaded and ready.

"Anyway, I made my way down there towards the creek as quietly as possible, not on the trail, but cutting through the woods so I wouldn't be seen, and the closer I got, the more I realized something bad was going on. I saw the horses first, with two strangers holding the reins of each of them. Then, I saw that there were several more of them, all men, and that they were all carrying guns that looked like military rifles. At first, I thought they might be soldiers, but they weren't in matching uniforms. Some of them were wearing green or tan clothing and some were in camouflage, but nothing that looked official. I finally saw Aaron when I moved a little closer, watching them from behind a big tree. Several of the men had him surrounded and were pointing their guns at him, and I counted a total of eleven of them. Aaron was on his knees and it looked like his hands were either tied or handcuffed behind his back.

"He was saying something to them and they seemed to be arguing back and forth with him and amongst themselves. I was terrified that they were going to shoot him, but then they pulled him up to his feet and made him go with them. I saw him turn and glance back up in the direction of the place where we were going to camp, and I know he was probably hoping that I was still up there, and that they wouldn't find me. I wanted to do something to help him, but I knew if those men saw me that they would come after me and if they caught me, I'd never be able to do anything for Aaron. They were taking him and the two horses away, but they apparently thought he was alone and had no idea they were being watched.

"They headed south, along the main trail in the direction we had been going. I knew I had to follow them, and that there was no time to go back and get my backpack or any of my gear or food because they might turn off the trail and then I'd never find them. So that's what I did, but I stayed way back, several hundred feet behind the two leading our horses, that were at the rear of the group. It was probably two miles and then we came to a road that crossed the trail. It was just gravel, like most of the roads up there, and I knew it was probably a forest service road. They turned right onto it and kept going, and I followed them, but I had to stay a lot farther back on the road than I did on the trail. They kept going even after it got dark, but within another hour or so, I could see campfires up ahead and I heard more voices. A lot more. I circled through the woods near the side of the road and tried to get a better look. There were lots of different campfires and a bunch of big tents. I couldn't tell how many people were there, but I knew it was a lot. I didn't know what they had done with Aaron, but I knew he was in that camp somewhere, and I wasn't about to leave him there if I could figure out a way to get him out.

"It was freezing cold after dark though and I didn't have my sleeping bag and of course, I couldn't build a fire. I knew I had to do something to stay warm, so I moved farther back in the woods, away from the camp and found a big fallen log I could get part of the way under. I piled spruce branches up against it to keep out the wind and crawled in there to wait until morning. I thought I was going to freeze to death, but as soon as it was daylight, I knew I had to sneak back there and try and see if I could spot Aaron.

"When it got lighter and I could see all of the camp, I saw that they had one big tent that was surrounded by razor wire like a prison and I knew that was probably where they'd put him. I found out I was right after I had been watching for a couple of hours and saw him and some other people walking around inside the wire. They had made Aaron a prisoner, but I had no idea why. All I knew was that these people weren't with the military and they had no right to hold him like that. The more I watched them, the more I began to realize that they were up to something, and I knew that they were trouble-makers or terrorists of some kind, and that they had set up their camp there because the area was remote and hard to get to. I realized they must have made Aaron and the others there either prisoners or hostages for some reason. Whatever they were going to do, I knew it was impossible for me to help Aaron alone. I hated to leave him there, but I knew he wouldn't want me to get caught too, and I was afraid if I stayed close to that place for too long, I would be.

"So, I left and went back to where we'd left the saddles and the other gear. I put all the food I could carry in my backpack and then I studied the maps we had to try and find the nearest main road, which was this one. I knew if all the stories I'd heard were true, that I would find an official checkpoint on it somewhere, and when I saw your vehicles parked across it, I got as close as I could on the ridge up there and watched until I was sure you were really with the actual military."

The sergeant listened to her entire story without interruption, but she couldn't read his expressionless face, and when she was finished, she didn't know whether he believed anything she'd just told him or not. "I can draw you a map of the exact spot where they are," she said. "I made careful mental notes of all the turns I made on the way out after I gathered my stuff. It's at the end of an actual road, so it's not that hard to find, it's just that it looks like it was a seldom-used road even before things turned out as they did."

"We're aware of a group of insurgents operating out of the backcountry up there," the sergeant said. "We think they're the same group that attacked and raided a national guard convoy several months ago. One reason we're here is to control access to and from those mountain areas, but we haven't been given authorization or the resources to actively hunt them down. Your information is interesting though, and I'll pass it along to my commanding officer."

"That's it? What about Aaron and the other prisoners? Those people may kill them if something's not done soon!"

"I understand your concern, Miss. But I don't get to make those kinds of decisions. All I can do is pass the information along, and yes, if you want to sketch out a map of what you know, I could use that too."

"And then what? What am I supposed to do now? I can't go back there alone."

"No. You don't need to be traveling anywhere alone. It's not only dangerous, but unauthorized personnel entering restricted areas is forbidden. You did the right thing, coming directly to my post and explaining your situation, because if you'd been seen trying to go around the checkpoint, you would have been arrested or shot. Since you've provided me with some potentially useful intel though, I will see if I can pull some strings and keep you out of the nearest refugee center. Is there someplace you'd like to go instead, if I can arrange transportation?"

FOURTEEN

A<small>ARON</small> S<small>ANTOS</small> <small>WOKE TO THE ROAR OF AUTOMATIC</small>
gunfire and explosions, seemingly coming from all direc-
tions at once. He was already sleeping on the floor of the
big tent, so there was nowhere to go that would get him
any lower, but he rolled over on his belly anyway and
flattened himself to the ground as much as possible. He
had no idea what time it was, as he'd been asleep until it
started, but he could tell it was still dark out despite the
flashes from the explosions and the fires that were
already burning in the encampment. Aaron heard
screams too along with the gunfire, and the sound of men
shouting in confusion and fear. It only took him a few
seconds to realize that his captors were under attack, and
that it was a major attack at that. How long that first
fusillade lasted, he had no idea, as he lost all sense of
time while he waited to see what was going to happen
next. Like the others confined in the tent with him, there

was little else Aaron could do. He had no weapons, and there was no escaping the razor-wire enclosure outside the tent, especially not with bullets flying everywhere, some of them striking his companions inside as well.

Aaron screamed at them to all stay down, but some didn't listen. He crawled to the far end where the two girls were and called out to Colleen. She answered and said she was okay, but the other one, whose name was Pamela, had been hit. Colleen was bent over her, trying to stop the bleeding, but when Aaron felt his way to them in the dark, he soon found himself in a pool of blood. He reached to help Colleen stop the flow, but Pamela had taken a round through the chest and nothing was going to help her now.

"WE'RE ALL GONNA DIE!" Colleen screamed.

Aaron didn't try to dispute it. It certainly seemed that way as the screams and gunshots continued for several more intense minutes. But eventually the shooting seemed to taper off, and through the canvas walls of the tent, Aaron could see bright lights sweeping the area of the camp outside. He heard men barking orders, and now and then the occasional single rifle or pistol shot that he assumed meant survivors were being finished off as they were found. Were he and his fellow prisoners going to be next? Aaron felt sure that was likely but when several of the attackers entered the tent, they held their fire. He and Colleen and the handful of others that were unhurt were ordered outside. Aaron could now see dozens of heavily armed soldiers moving throughout the camp, many of them setting fires to the other tents as well as the vehicles and stacks of supplies.

Aaron was fairly certain that the men in this attacking force were regular government troops. They wore matching battle uniforms and were much more disciplined and methodical than the men who'd been holding them. That didn't mean they were necessarily safe now though, and Aaron was certain that he and Colleen and the other survivors would be held, and then no doubt taken away to be processed into one of the detainment camps. There was no way Aaron could let that happen. Megan had been alone out there in the wilderness as far as he knew for the entire time he'd been here, which was going on two weeks now. She had apparently managed to stay out of sight when he was captured, but he had no idea what she'd done next, although he'd hoped that she would try to continue on south to his people's land. She had the maps and he'd discussed the route with her at great length. If she did make it, there was no guarantee they would let an outsider in though, and that was why Aaron knew he had to escape and get on the trail for home as quickly as possible. He was thinking fast as he looked down at his blood-soaked clothes; blood that had sprayed on him and Colleen when he was trying to save Pamela. Aaron had wiped most of it off of his hands, but now he clutched at his side and grimaced in pain, telling the soldier nearest him that he'd been hit, and that he needed help.

"Can you walk?" The man asked, glancing at his bloody shirt.

"Yes. The bullet just went through my side. But it's bleeding a lot. Is there a medic with you?"

"Yeah, follow me. We'll find him."

Aaron squeezed Colleen's hand and gave her a smile before he left. He doubted he'd ever see her again unless he failed, but failure wasn't an option. Megan was his priority and Colleen would probably survive whatever was in store for her with or without him. But Megan might not if he didn't get out of this place fast. Aaron followed the soldier, relieved to see that the man trusted him enough to lead the way rather than force him at gunpoint like the militia guys had. That confirmed his assumption that he wasn't their prisoner too, but he was also quite certain he wouldn't be allowed to just walk away to wherever he wanted to go. The other good thing was that it was still dark, even though he knew it wouldn't be for long. Aaron scanned the rest of the camp around him as he followed along, pretending to hold pressure on his non-existent wound in order to stop the bleeding. All the soldiers he could see were busy. They were checking the dead for weapons and gathering up whatever supplies were not going in the burn piles. Since the camp was practically already in the edge of the woods, Aaron knew he wouldn't have to make it far to be out of sight and back in his element. He slowed his pace to create some distance between him and the man leading him, and then he turned and bolted as fast as he could run, aiming at the darkest shadows he could spot beyond the perimeter.

He heard someone else shout out an alarm and then an order for him to stop, but Aaron didn't slow down and didn't look back. If a bullet cut him down for his efforts, then so be it, but he wasn't going to be taken away to some other camp by these soldiers. He flinched when he heard two gunshots in rapid succession but felt nothing and heard no whiz of bullets going past his ears, and seconds later, the dark forest had swallowed him up. Aaron didn't know whether the soldiers would come after him or not since he wasn't one of the enemy, but he was taking no chances by slowing down. If they did search for him, they had the advantage with their bright lights and probably night vision equipment as well. Aaron's only chance was to put as much distance between himself and the camp as possible, but he was also aware of keeping his bearings too. He'd fled the camp heading west, which was nothing but roadless wilderness, but he knew he would have to circle back to the north and then east in order to return to the trail where he'd last seen Megan.

It was a good thing he *wasn't* actually wounded, Aaron thought, because his good health and fitness were all he had. He'd thought to put on his shoes when the shooting first started, in case there was an opportunity to run, but other than that and the clothes on his back, Aaron had nothing but his skills to help him survive. It was bitter cold in the predawn dark, but the steep uphill hike out of the valley and away from the camp warmed him enough until the morning sun knocked back the chill. By that time, Aaron was confident that the soldiers weren't in pursuit. He figured one refugee wasn't worth the bother to them, as their mission had obviously been to eradicate the militia camp. Aaron wondered what those men who'd captured him had done to bring down the wrath of the Army, but he'd seen this on a lesser scale when Gareth and some of the other idiots from the resistance camp had shot up that supply convoy. How they thought they'd get away with it was beyond Aaron, and he had successfully convinced Megan that it was time to get away from that maniac. Colleen had filled him in on what happened next though, telling him about how Gareth talked her and Brett, as well as Jeremy into coming after them. She didn't know what happened to Gareth and the others, but it was their fault she'd ended up held hostage by the militia. Aaron hoped that Gareth got what he deserved, just as their former captors had, but he figured he would never know, so he gave it little more thought. His task for today was to get back to the rock overhang where he'd last seen Megan. It took him until late afternoon because of the circuitous route he deemed necessary to avoid being seen, and when he got there, he found what he'd expected.

Megan was long gone, of course, but the two saddles and some of the packs were still there, tucked away behind the rocks so that anyone that wasn't specifically looking for them would pass by without seeing them.

She'd taken only her backpack, which was the reasonable thing to do, along with as much of the food as she could carry. She'd taken most of the foods that could be eaten without cooking, things like the nuts and peanut butter and jerky. But she'd left their cooking pot and bags of rice and some of the canned beans and other non-perishables. Aaron quickly opened a can and scarfed down some of the beans. He was starving from putting down all those hard miles, not to mention he hadn't been fed well the entire time he was being held.

Megan had taken the .45 auto pistol that Vicky's grandpa had given them, and Aaron was glad to see that she had. His rifle had been taken from him when he was captured, and they'd been carrying no other firearms, so he was going to have to continue south unarmed, but at least she'd left some of his other gear behind. His sleeping bag was there, as well as his jacket, and digging through the packs he found a large pocketknife she'd probably overlooked. Aaron had hoped she would leave him a note or something, but of course she hadn't, and he knew it was probably because she had witnessed what happened and had no reason to believe he would escape to return to this place. He was glad she had the wisdom not to try and interfere when he was captured, because it would have surely led to her capture too, but he knew she must have been devastated at the prospect of being left out there alone with no way to help him. Aaron had emphatically told her when they first left that she was to go on without him if something happened to him along the way, and that was why he'd given her the details of where to go and who to talk to on the reservation. He just hoped she'd done as he asked, because they'd already come so far, and she had nowhere else to go unless she turned back to the ranch. Considering that possibility, Aaron backtracked a bit on the trail to the north before it got too dark to see, looking for tracks or any other sign Megan had gone back. When he found nothing, he went back to the rock overhang to get some sleep. He would continue looking as he made his way south, hoping he would catch up to her before she reached the reservation boundary, or she fell into the hands of men like those who'd captured him.

When he began his journey the next morning, Aaron had rigged one of the saddlebags to serve as a backpack, loading it with all of the remaining food Megan had left behind. He would still have to find more along the way, considering how far he had to walk, but Aaron wasn't overly concerned about that. He would be crossing trout streams along the way, and there was always the possibility of taking small game like rabbit or grouse with a well-aimed rock or simple throwing stick. Aaron knew he could do this because he'd practiced it before when roaming the backcountry with his uncle and cousins. He was much more worried about Megan, attempting a hike like that alone. Even if it weren't for the threat of being attacked, the mountain wilderness held so many dangers for someone so inexperienced and ill-equipped, especially this time of year. His only hope that she might

survive the trek was that they had spent many hours
discussing the various what-if scenarios and he'd done his
best to teach her as much as she could absorb in the short
time they'd been traveling together.

Perhaps the most serious danger he'd emphasized to
her was the storms that could hit the mountains this time
of year. Getting caught at higher elevations could be
fatal, and just two days after resuming his journey, Aaron
had to follow his own advice and leave the trail for the
shelter of a heavily-forested drainage on the east side of
the divide. The snow was enough to close all the higher
passes, forcing him to seek alternate routes that took him
days out of his way. The extra travel time guaranteed
that the food he was carrying wouldn't last, but Aaron
pushed on, reducing his eating to the minimum necessary to keep walking. Every day he saw mule deer that
would have been easy pickings if he'd but had a rifle, but
there was no point in wishing for the impossible. Aaron
instead spent an afternoon at a small stream crossing
stocking up on trout that he found in the deeper pools
among the rocks. He missed many more than he
managed to impale on the spear he carved from a small
sapling, but even so, he soon procured more than he
could eat, splitting the rest and hanging them on racks he
built near the fire, so they would dry, and he could take
them with him.

Aaron had always been fascinated with the reputa-
tion his ancestors had for living off the land. While all
the Native Americans had lived close to the land in the

days before the Europeans came, the Apache were particularly adept at surviving in even the harshest regions of the inhospitable southwest. And they could do it while traveling great distances and raiding and fighting. Aaron knew all the stories of the legendary Apache war chiefs like Geronimo and Cochise, and how they defied the entire U.S. Army even when operating in small bands of just a handful of warriors. Aaron knew it was that intimacy with the land that allowed them to do it. They didn't need to be burdened with supplies to cover great distances, because they knew how to find food and water in places no outsider could. Aaron had always wanted to be like that, but no Apache he knew in modern times really was. His uncle was as close as anyone he'd ever met, and he had taught Aaron a lot when he was growing up on the reservation, but most of the old ways and skills were forgotten, and few of the youth could care less anyway. Aaron certainly cared though, and even if he could never be like those warriors of old, he was justifiably proud of himself as he sat there by the fire with his catch, traveling the same country they'd surely roamed as he drew closer to what was now the Colorado-New Mexico border.

Aaron wondered now if he'd made a terrible mistake talking Megan into leaving with him to go to his tribal lands. Had he done it out of pure selfishness, because he had a crush on her and wanted to be with her? Aaron didn't want to think so, but if he didn't find her there—if something happened to her out in this wilderness—then who's fault was it but his? She had already told him that even if she did go with him to the reservation, she had no intention of staying there long-term. He kept believing she would change her mind though, once they were there, and give up on the foolish idea of trying to travel all the way to south Florida after all that had happened. If even part of what they'd heard about the hurricane that hit there at the end of summer was true, then Aaron doubted there'd be anything left for her to go home to. He knew she didn't want to think about it, but there was a good possibility her mother and her stepfather and stepbrother were dead. And if they weren't, how would she get there and how would she ever find them? But when they left the ranch together, Aaron had told her that he would do everything he could to help her figure that out if it was what she wanted.

At least New Mexico was one step closer, he'd said. And the reservation lands would likely provide them some insulation from what was going on out in the rest of the surrounding countryside. Aaron felt sure that the tribal council would mobilize and add more police or form a tribal militia to protect their people and land. He doubted the government forces would interfere so long as the people kept to themselves, and the others fighting to bring down the country would have no quarrel with the natives, nor would there be much of value on reservation land to attract the opportunists. Aaron was confident the reservation was one of the safest places in the entire region in which to take refuge, and he'd convinced

Megan of the same. But now he'd failed her by foolishly letting his guard down, leaving her alone in a wilderness with no way of knowing that he was free again and back on route to their planned destination. He hoped that Megan somehow made it there before him, but if she had, what was she going to tell the people? All she had was his name and the names of his aunt and uncle. Aaron didn't know if they would believe her or not when she told them what happened, and even if they did, he doubted his uncle or anyone else from the reservation would be able to go and try and find him. And even though Megan didn't know where they'd taken him or how many other armed men were in that camp, she had to know that it would take more help than just his uncle to rescue him, and Aaron really doubted the tribal council would authorize such an expedition off the reservation given the circumstances. He hoped they wouldn't, of course, because he wouldn't be there anyway now, and his captors were all dead, but the real question was whether Megan ever got there or not at all.

Aaron reached the reservation boundary some two weeks later. He didn't have any I.D. on him as the men who'd taken him captive had stripped him of his wallet after they took his rifle and searched him for other weapons. Aaron wasn't worried though, because he knew a backdoor route that would take him into the area where his uncle's land was located. The canyon trail was far from any of the roads entering the reservation and there was no water along the route, so it was seldom used.

Aaron's uncle had taken him there several times to show him some ancient sites where the people who'd inhabited the canyon long before the Apache had left their stories painted on the rocks. Aaron paused to look at them for a moment and to give thanks that he had made it back to the lands of his people.

When he reached the low sandstone bluff over-looking the adobe dwelling belonging to his uncle, Daisy, the black and white border collie that watched over the place spotted him and began barking immediately. Aaron called out to her as he made his way down, and once she verified his identity with her nose, she rushed out to greet him, jumping up onto him like they did this every day. Aaron gave her some attention for a moment and then looked past her to the closed front door of the house. He knew if his Uncle Ethan or Aunt Ava were home, they would have heard Daisy's barking, but no one opened the door, and when he walked around to the front of the house, he saw that his uncle's newer Dodge truck was gone, but the old rusted-out Toyota 4x4 was still parked out by the road. Aaron knocked on the door anyway to be sure no one was inside, and when he got no response, he reached up to feel over the top of one of the front window frames for the hidden key.

When he went inside, he could tell they hadn't been away long. There was a covered pot of beans on the stove, still slightly warm to the touch, and a big stack of corn tortillas wrapped in a cloth. Aaron was so hungry he didn't even bother sitting down to eat. He found a spoon and began piling beans on tortillas one after another until he was afraid it would make him sick if he kept stuffing his empty stomach. Aunt Ava might pretend to be mad at him at first, but she wouldn't mind in the end, and Aaron was sure they would be back soon, or she wouldn't have left dirty dishes in the sink. He walked down the hall to the open door of the bedroom where he always stayed when he came to visit and stopped in his tracks at what he saw inside. *It seemed impossible, but Megan's backpack was laying there open on the foot of the unmade bed!*

Aaron crossed the room and picked it up to examine it to be sure. It was Megan's all right, the same one she'd had since leaving the campus with Vicky and Gareth, and he recognized some of her things inside it as well as one of her shirts draped over the wooden chair in the bedroom, leaving him with no doubt that she'd been there very recently, maybe even that morning. *Megan had made it all the way to the reservation on her own!* Aaron was ecstatic and amazed. He put the backpack back on the bed and went outside, looking down the desolate dusty road that stretched south to the horizon. There was no sign of a vehicle, not even a plume of dust on that distant plain, but Aaron figured they must have gone to the store in Dulce or somewhere else nearby. He figured they would probably be back later that day, but Aaron was too impatient to wait. He went out to the old Toyota and looked under the floor mat for the key and found it still there. Aaron prayed the old truck would fire up as the starter slowly began to grind, with barely enough juice in the battery to turn over the engine. He stopped before he drained it completely and pumped the gas pedal for one last try. This time the engine sputtered to life, idling roughly, but running, and Aaron put it in gear and drove off.

FIFTEEN

ONCE HE MADE HIS DECISION, ERIC SET A PACE THAT kept both him and the horses at the edge of exhaustion. Most of the miles he covered in the dark, when it was safer to use the faster Jeep trails and other remote roads that paralleled the divide. He stopped anytime the route took him across a particularly exposed open area, scanning the rocks and surrounding slopes for signs of militia or military patrols. But as far as he could tell, he was the only one braving the nighttime cold. It wasn't pleasant, by any means, but Eric had a goal and he was used to being uncomfortable. He was getting used to the advantages and disadvantages of the horses too and learning to adapt to planning around their requirements for water, feeding and rest. On the one hand, it was frustrating having to deal with them, but the upside was that he could cover more ground when he was moving and do so with a lot more weight in the form of food as well as his weapons and ammunition. Traveling this way seemed fitting in the landscape he rode through, and Eric felt bad for Bob Barham, whose horses he was now using and whose dreams of a journey like this came to an end with a single load of buckshot.

It was a sad ending for Bob but considering all Eric had encountered since he'd slipped away from that cabin alone, Eric knew he had absolutely done the right thing. There was no way he would have gotten as far or learned as much as he had with Shauna, Vicky and Jonathan tagging along, and he hoped like hell they'd done as he asked and stayed put. He knew Jonathan probably would if it were up to him, but Shauna's stubbornness still worried him. He didn't want to think about what would happen if she ran into another bunch of those militia guys, waiting to bushwhack travelers using the trail. It was hard to put it out of his mind, but he kept hoping that Jonathan and Vicky were able to convince her of the wisdom of waiting when she showed them the letter. Eric knew she'd probably ripped it to shreds shortly after, probably while calling him every name in the book, but Jonathan was still unable to walk, and Vicky was dealing with the emotions of having killed a man, and one that had once been her roommate's boyfriend. Neither of those two would be keen on facing more hardships and danger when they had a better alternative and Eric's sound reasoning for waiting laid out in his own handwriting. Shauna might sulk and fume, but if she were outvoted, Eric doubted she'd attempt to follow him alone.

But Shauna wouldn't wait there indefinitely unless the snowfall was so heavy it was impossible to leave. Eric had to move fast to find out if Megan and Aaron had made it to that reservation, because if they hadn't, then his search was going to take him into even greater danger and into places he could never bring three civilians with all that was going on. He calculated he could reach the northern boundary of the Jicarilla reservation in 10 days or so from the site of the massacre, but he also knew from looking at the map that the reservation encompassed a vast area of land, much of it as empty-looking as the national forests he was now traversing. He had no idea on which part of it Aaron's relatives lived, but he knew the boy's last name was Santos, and he hoped that would be a start. He would have to make contact with someone there when he arrived, but he didn't expect he would be met with a warm welcome as an outsider seeking to enter tribal lands. If someone in authority there was willing to hear him out, it was more likely they'd listen if he weren't accompanied by what appeared to be an entire family of white folks seeking asylum on Apache lands. And the other advantage of going alone was that he could infiltrate by whatever means necessary if that seemed more prudent when he got there than asking permission.

Along the way, of course, Eric had to cross multiple highways and paved county roads, each of them a danger point that he had to scope out carefully before picking the most direct route across that would minimize his exposure. Most of these he crossed in the darkness. No one was traveling those roads at night, but he did have to make a wide detour around a stopped convoy he encountered in a stretch of high desert just north of the state line. The divide trail ran south from the San Juan National Forest in Colorado to Carson National Forest in northern New Mexico, but the reservation lands lay to the west of those public lands, and to get there, Eric had to pick a route that was part cross-country and partly on backroads. Water for himself and for the horses became one of his biggest concerns, and Eric located it by watching for the surviving cattle he found on the ranch land he passed through, taking care to use only the stock tanks he found well clear of any houses that may or may not still be inhabited.

From the direction he was traveling, the transition from the surrounding public lands to Jicarilla Apache lands was imperceptible. Eric was able to estimate his position by dead-reckoning using a peak that was visible to the east and also appeared on the best map he had of the area, but on this side of the reservation, there were no main roads or checkpoints. He crossed what he thought was the boundary through a barbed wire fence that stretched to the horizon in both directions, but Eric saw neither Apaches nor anyone else in all that emptiness. While one option would have been to circle around the reservation boundary until he came to a road where he might find an actual checkpoint, Eric decided instead to take his chances with seeking out the inhabitants within, in hopes of finding someone who knew Aaron Santos and his relatives who lived there.

He felt better about his chances of covering ground undetected when the desert plain transitioned to juniper and pinion covered hills. Eric found a live spring in the bottom of what he first thought was a dry gulch, and feeling that he was well-hidden there, decided to give the horses a chance to graze and rest. Looking over the area carefully, he saw no footprints or other signs of human activity and assumed it was because he was still a long way from the inhabited parts of the reservation. As he sat there watching the horses, Eric debated about whether he should leave them there where they had access to water and go on alone on foot to lessen the chances of being seen. The last thing he wanted to do, however, was to come across as an enemy, sneaking onto Apache lands with a weapon in hand. Thinking about how that might end up, Eric decided that in the morning he would ride on in the daylight, and when he was confronted, as he inevitably would be, he could claim ignorance, saying he hadn't seen any signs and didn't know that he was in a restricted area. That strategy would at least buy him time to talk, and he hoped that when he began name dropping, they would be ready to listen.

Eric crawled into his sleeping bag, stretched onto a patch of sand between several big rocks, on the rim of the shallow gulch, leaving the horses hobbled some 50 feet below, where they were concealed by the cottonwoods that grew near the spring. Before turning in to catch up on all his lost sleep, Eric had climbed up to the top of a nearby rock that afforded him an unobstructed view of the surrounding hills, and he felt confident that he was indeed alone there. The horses seemed content and at peace as well, and Eric fell asleep feeling good about his prospects for tomorrow. It wasn't the warm rays of the morning sun that woke him, however. When Eric opened his eyes, the brilliance of the Milky Way galaxy stretching across the desert sky was the first thing he saw, although it wasn't starlight that intruded on his sleep either. Eric woke because some sixth sense told him something was wrong, and the instant he turned his eyes to the chunk of wood beside him, upon which he propped his M4 before zipping up his bag, Eric knew it wasn't his imagination. *The rifle was gone!* He reached for the Glock that was still inside the sleeping bag with him and was out of the bag and crouching beside one of the big rocks in an instant. A quick scan around him confirmed that all his other gear was gone as well... his saddle, saddlebags, the other rifles, food, water, maps... *all of it!* Eric remained frozen in place, listening for anything that might give away the unseen thief that had taken his gear, but the desert was silent. He listened for sounds from the horses down below but heard nothing. After several more minutes of waiting, Eric decided that if whoever did this wanted him dead, they could have easily killed him while he slept if they were good enough to get that close and get away with his stuff undetected.

He crawled closer to the rim of the gulch and looked down into the shadows of the trees for any sign of the horses, but they were gone too! *Dammit!*

Eric knew what it was like to sneak into an enemy camp at night, but the times he'd done it usually resulted in taking out or capturing the targets. It took even more nerve to pull off something like this without firing a shot or using a blade. What really puzzled Eric was how they knew he was there, and he began to wonder now how long he'd been observed the previous day. The landscape he'd ridden through had appeared uninhabited, but someone was clearly out there, and now they had most of his stuff and were apparently long gone. He knew better than to assume an attack wasn't yet to come, but as he remained low there among the rocks listening and waiting, he began to wonder whether it was simply his gear and his horses that the nighttime intruders wanted. Eric had no doubt they were native to the reservation though, and he figured there must be a dwelling somewhere nearby in the brush-covered hills that he hadn't noticed.

He knew someone out there in the dark might have him in their rifle sights at that very moment, but it was a chance he was willing to take. He stuffed his sleeping bag back into its sack and with that in one hand and the Glock in the other, made his way down to the bottom of the gulch to be sure the horses were truly gone. After a bit of searching, he found evidence in an area of sand illuminated enough by starlight to make out hoof prints. They led away from the gulch directly opposite from where he'd been sleeping, heading south in the direction he planned to go anyway. Since Eric had little other option but to keep going, that's what he did. He didn't know if he'd ever see his horses or his other things again, but he was still hopeful he could find someone on the reservation that would hear him out.

He covered several more miles uneventfully, winding his way south through the hills and then along another dry drainage until dawn broke, and the weird, laughing-like yip of a coyote nearby in the brush ahead caught his attention. Eric thought little of it until he heard another one echo practically the same call from behind him, in the direction opposite. It raised his suspicions a little, but when he didn't hear again, he dismissed it and moved on. But he'd only walked another half mile or so when he heard more coyote sounds from up ahead, answered again by the others that were apparently following him. Eric spun around, looking for the best escape route but stopped when he saw three figures emerge from the scrub. All were pointing rifles at him and a glance over his shoulder confirmed that he was surrounded, as four more of the two-legged 'coyotes' now materialized from that direction, those pointing rifles as well. Eric kept the Glock lowered at his side as the seven men closed in on him. They were wearing desert tan camo, and most were carrying AKs, although he recognized his own M4 in the hands of one of them. That they were Apache security forces or militia of some kind was without question, even before the first one spoke. All of these men were dark-skinned and black-haired, and all but one of them wore their hair long, in the traditional manner. Two of the long-haired ones even had a band of what appeared to be white war paint running horizontally across their faces, just below the eyes. It was one of those that spoke first:

"Drop your weapon and step away from it, white man! You are trespassing on Jicarilla lands!"

"I understand," Eric said, letting the pistol fall from his hands.

"STEP BACK! DO IT NOW!"

Eric took a couple of steps back and then three of the men rushed in, one grabbing the pistol and the other two shoving their rifle barrels into his body, pushing him back further.

"I know I'm trespassing," Eric said, "but I am looking for someone who lives here."

Eric felt the sharp jab of one of the rifles thrust into his ribs and then the other one slammed the wooden butt of his AK into his upper thigh. Before he could react, two more men were upon him from behind, sweeping him off of his feet and slamming him hard onto the dusty ground. Guns were at his head as he was rolled over, his hands pulled behind his back. Eric felt steel handcuffs tighten around his wrists before he was roughly rolled back the other way.

"You came onto our lands yesterday with rifles, that pistol, and even a grenade launcher and grenades! Who are you with, white man? Are you a member of one of those militias that want to take away even the little land

207

we have left? Or are you a soldier, sent here to gather information to help the government do the same thing?"

"I'm neither one!" Eric said. "I'm alone and I work for no one! I'm looking for my daughter and her friend, and this reservation is the last place they were headed."

"Well, the only place *you're* headed is to jail. But only long enough to be interrogated. When we find out who you really are and who sent you, you'll pay the price for violating the laws of the sovereign Jicarilla Apache Nation!"

Eric knew the window to escape or fight was closed. He'd screwed up royally and now he was at the mercy of these men. He could tell by the way several of his captors handled their weapons and operated that they'd gotten their training in combat, probably in Special Ops like himself. Those that had firsthand experience with war overseas had likely served as trainers here at home. Like so many other groups, the Jicarilla were mobilizing to protect and defend their own against the insanity raging around the country. These men were proud to carry on the warrior tradition of their ancestors, and judging from what he'd seen of them, they were doing a damned fine job of it.

He saw his horses again when one of the men went to get their own mounts, Eric was helped into the saddle and then the little band set out for their tribal militia headquarters, in a small community 10 miles to the south. Eric was locked in a jail cell without further questioning that first day and given no food, only a small jug of water. As far as he could tell, he was the only one in lockup there, which didn't necessarily bode well. Like tribal councils he'd encountered in Afghanistan and several countries in Africa, Eric imagined these guys administered judgement and carried out sentences swiftly and efficiently. Death was the expected outcome for falling into the hands of men such as these in times of war. Eric knew that all too well.

When the time came to talk the following day, his interrogator asked the same questions over and over, striking him with heavy blows each time Eric didn't tell him what he wanted to hear. He was being charged with trespassing, espionage and terrorism, all as he expected, and they wanted to know the details of his mission and who had sent him. And Eric kept saying over and over that the only reason he was here was because he believed his daughter was coming here with her Apache friend. All Eric knew about the boy was his name, and that he'd been a student at the university Megan attended in Boulder. Eric had nothing else to tell them, and no other way to prove he was who he said he was, even when he said that yes, he had been in the military years prior, but no, he was no longer in the service. Eric knew the possession of two select-fire M4s and a grenade launcher didn't help his story, but on the other hand, reasonable men did not go about unarmed in the present environment. He apologized for entering Jicarilla land without first finding a checkpoint and asking permission. The stone-cold, expressionless face of his interrogator made him doubt any of that would make the slightest difference in determining his fate.

Eric was taken back to his cell, but he didn't expect to be held long, one way or the other. He'd made a major operational mistake by underestimating the security forces here, and this time there was no team or anyone else coming to break him out. No one even knew he was here, other than the three people he'd left behind in that cabin in Colorado, and if they had done what he asked, they were waiting there still. That's why it came as a surprise when the guard came to his cell the next day to tell him he had visitors. When the door was unlocked with only one guard present and no handcuffs on his wrists, Eric knew this might be his last chance to fight for his freedom or even his life. He could take the guard easily, but the man seemed unconcerned with him, as if he were no longer considered a threat. Eric decided to wait at least long enough to see what this was about and learn who it was that wished to see him here, of all places.

SIXTEEN

After Megan's conversation with the sergeant at the highway checkpoint, she was taken to a small office in the portable building and told she would have to wait there until he cleared his request with his superiors. She was still in disbelief at his offer to try and secure her transportation, as she came here worried that she would be sent away to one of the refugee centers or worse if she couldn't convince them her story was true. It was the little details she sprinkled here and there that did the trick though, especially some of the operational lingo she'd learned from her dad. And the sergeant knew she wasn't lying about being the daughter of a Navy SEAL when she told him a few stories she knew of Eric Branson's exploits during the years he was fighting in Afghanistan.

After that, she had been moved by truck to a larger post about an hour to the east, and there she waited for several days while the arrangements were being made. No one could tell her whether or not any actions were going to be taken in regard to the information she'd given them about the militia camp. It was a helpless feeling, knowing she couldn't do anything else for Aaron, other than wait and see, but at least his family was going to know what had happened in the meantime. The choice to go there to the reservation rather than ask for help reaching Florida was an easy one for Megan. She still wanted to go home, of course, and she was determined to do so when she could. But Aaron had risked his life to help her reach that goal, and the least she could do was make the effort to tell his uncle and aunt what happened and wait long enough to see if he might be rescued.

The trip to the reservation was the end of her contact with the soldiers, and there had been no promise that she could change her mind later and go back to ask for help again. She waited in the truck while the officer in charge of her escort talked with the tribal police manning the gate, and the only thing that got her in was the good fortune that one of the Apache officers knew Aaron's uncle personally. Megan told him her story in detail once she was inside, and then she had another day and a half wait until someone could drive her out to Ethan Santos' remote homestead. The aunt and uncle turned out to be as kind and generous as Aaron had said they were though. They welcomed her into their home and thanked her profusely for coming all that way to bring them the news of what had happened to Aaron. But

Megan felt bad that she was the one that escaped rather than their beloved nephew.

"You did the right thing," Ethan said. "You were smart to stay out of sight of those men, and brave to follow them so that you would know where they took Aaron. No one would ever know what happened if you had been taken too."

"I know, but I just feel terrible that I couldn't *do* something. I hated to leave him there, but I had no choice."

"You found the soldiers and told them. That was something. I don't think they would care about a few hostages, but you said that sergeant was already interested in that militia group?"

"Yes, he seemed really interested. That's why he was so nice to me and arranged for me to come here. I think they *will* do something. He seemed like a good man."

"Maybe, but if they do something, it will not be because of my nephew. My people have a long history of mistrust for government soldiers, and even though that is in the past, I still doubt the Army will bother with anything that isn't a high-value target for them, and it may take them a long time to decide to act. I will talk to some of the other men in my family. If we don't hear anything soon, then we will go there to this place you described and get Aaron ourselves."

For the first time since leaving Vicky's grandparents' ranch, Megan felt she was truly safe. In fact, she felt much safer here than at the ranch because she didn't have to deal with Gareth. The longer she was around that guy, the scarier he seemed, and she simply could no longer trust him. It bothered her that she had fallen for him in the first place, but he was such a smooth talker that he had really taken her in before she knew what was happening. She really hoped he had moved on with his friends and not stayed there to give Vicky and her sweet grandparents any grief. Megan felt bad about leaving Vicky with Gareth still there, but there was little else she could do at the time. Now she was safe because of Aaron but feeling really guilty too, because she was the one here with his aunt and uncle instead of him. It seemed that everything she did caused someone else to suffer or be put in danger. Megan was glad she came here though, because she really believed that Ethan and any other men he could recruit from the reservation would go and try to find Aaron. He was one of their own after all, and Ethan assured her that the Jicarilla were sticking together now like they hadn't in more than a hundred years. Ethan and Ava told Megan that she was welcome to stay there at their house for as long as she wanted. Even if he left to go look for Aaron, she could stay, but he understood if she wanted to try and make it home to Florida.

"No. If you go to Colorado to look for him, then I want to go too," Megan said. "You need me because I can show you exactly where that camp is located, and besides, I would be worried the whole time I was waiting here. It would drive me crazy."

"If we go, it is likely there will be a battle at the end

of our journey, Megan. You have been through enough already, and Aaron would not want you to take such a risk. But we will have a few days to talk about it. It will take that long to organize and get ready."

The planning didn't get far however, before a new development changed everything. One of Ethan's friends drove up to the place a few days later in his pickup, bringing a message from the tribal militia headquarters to the east. Megan couldn't help but overhear the conversation from the front porch as she sat in the kitchen with Ava, the door partially open.

"They captured a white intruder on tribal lands," the man told Ethan. "He was heavily armed and traveling alone on horseback, so naturally it was assumed that he was up to no good and sent here by someone. But after they beat the shit out of him and questioned him for two days, he still wouldn't tell them who he was with."

"So? Aren't they just going to hang him and be done with it?"

"Probably, but Nantan, my friend in the tribal council, told me something that the man kept repeating, and said I ought to come and let you know. He thought you'd be interested in hearing what this white man had to say, even if it is a lie."

"Me? Why would I care?"

"Because he claims he came here looking for you. Well, not by name, but he said he was looking for Aaron Santos' uncle. When they asked him why, he said it was because Aaron had been traveling with his daughter, and that he had reason to believe they were both headed here, to your place on the reservation."

Megan heard this and tried to make sense of it. Who could this man be, who thought Aaron was with his daughter? She knew Vicky's mom and dad were in Portland, so it seemed unlikely her dad could have made his way here. Unless it was Colleen's dad, there wasn't anyone else in their group that could be mistaken for her if they had heard that Aaron had left for the reservation with a female friend. Megan went outside, apologizing for butting into the conversation, but she had to ask, even though she didn't know Colleen's dad's name. "Do you know this white man's name?"

"Yeah, they said it was Branson. I believe they said *Eric* Branson. Do you know him?"

For a moment, Megan was speechless, but then she got herself together and told them that yes, her father's name was Eric Branson. Upon hearing this, Ethan said they would leave immediately to go and see this man who claimed to be him. The ride to the tribal militia headquarters seemed to take forever, with Megan seated in the front of Ethan's pickup with Ava beside her in the middle as she told them all about her dad from the moment they left. She was certain there must be some kind of mistake, because it was impossible that her dad could be here. Even if he actually came back to the U.S. to look for her, which she hadn't expected to happen, how would he possibly know she'd come here, of all places? Of course, she wanted to believe it, but it just seemed too far-fetched to make sense.

But the man that brought the news told them that this fellow they were holding wasn't just some random civilian. The tribal militia had captured him easily enough because they greatly outnumbered him and took him by surprise, but the interrogator could tell he had combat experience and training. And he was carrying weapons that weren't easy for civilians to come by, at least not before the anarchy started. Megan knew her dad had a look and a way of carrying himself that made it hard to hide the fact that he was a dangerous man, and he had the toughness and resolve to take whatever punishment that interrogator may have dished out. She hated to think that he might really be hurt though, just because he came here to find her, but she wasn't going to believe any of this was true until she saw him herself. Before she was allowed to do that though, she was taken into the headquarters of the tribal council and militia to answer questions about Eric Branson herself.

"So, your name is Megan? Where did you attend college, Megan, and where did you live before that?"

Megan answered truthfully, knowing they were checking her answers against whatever this man who claimed to be her father told them.

"And you were traveling here with Aaron Santos because he was your friend in college, but you arrived here in a U.S. Army truck, with a story about Aaron being captured by some militia group in the mountains in Colorado...."

Megan wondered what they were trying to get to, and for a moment thought this might be some kind of trick. Some of the men present had already heard her answer these questions before, when they interviewed her before letting her in when the military escort dropped her off. But she kept reminding herself that there was no way any of these people would know her father's name, and she didn't know how they would have gotten it. She continued to answer truthfully, providing all the details they asked for, including what she knew of her father's service. She told them that he was a Navy SEAL and which SEAL team he'd been a part of, and then she told them the names of two of the private security companies he'd worked for after he got out and began contracting. She didn't know the most current one, but she knew he had signed on with a company that had lots of assets in Europe.

"If he's here, it's only because he's looking for me," Megan said. "He didn't come back here to work for the American military or to contract for any militia, and even if he had, why would he be here on your lands? I just want to see him. If it's really him, you'll know he's my father when you see the look on his face when he sees me. Please! I've told you everything I know!"

Megan didn't know for sure what was going to happen next but the man asking questions nodded at one of his companions, who then left the room. It was several minutes later before the door opened again, and when it did, three men entered the room: the one who'd just left, a uniformed tribal police officer from the jail, *and her dad!* Megan nearly knocked her chair over getting to her feet she was so excited. And when he saw her there in the same room with him, his jaw dropped in disbelief. *It was true! The tribal militia really had caught Eric Branson sneaking onto Jicarilla land!*

Eric was immediately cleared of all charges against him by the Jicarilla tribal council after he and Megan each told their versions of how they were connected to Aaron Santos while sitting there together in the same room. When he'd first seen her, Eric had assumed that she and Aaron had made it there together as they'd set out to do. But hearing her tell the details of his capture and her subsequent meeting with the sergeant at that highway checkpoint, Eric immediately understood why he'd found that second militia camp completely destroyed.

"Of course they couldn't tell you, since you're a civilian and the conflict is ongoing, but you can bet that your intel gave them what they needed to make that strike. You did the right thing, Megan, and that took courage!"

But Eric knew this news left his daughter full of doubt as to Aaron's well-being. Upon hearing that he found so many dead, she wasn't convinced that Aaron wasn't among them.

"I'm certain that I didn't find anyone there that looked Native American, especially not anyone with long hair, and believe me, I looked, because Vicky gave me a good description. There must have been other hostages that were rescued, and we *will* find him, Megan, I promise you that! I'll go and find that sergeant you talked to and convince him to look into where they were taken."

Eric knew this wasn't enough to dispel Megan's worry though, and he understood why. Aaron could have been severely wounded in the attack and may have died later in transit to wherever they were taking survivors they rescued. A number of things could have happened to him, but the fact that the sergeant was able to finagle a ride to the reservation for Megan was promising. Eric figured they must have had a really good reason for wanting to know the location of that militia camp, and just as he'd thought when he first saw the devastation there, a really good reason for hitting it with such a hard and decisive strike. He was sure that there was a lot going on in this region that he didn't know about yet, and that made going anywhere dangerous, but he'd promised his daughter he would do all he could to find Aaron, and he intended to keep that promise.

"Aaron is a great guy," Megan assured him. "He said that if I came here with him, I could stay as long as I wanted, but he knew I wanted to try and get back to

Florida where Mom is, and he said he would do anything he could to help me. Now I've got to help him first, but after I know he's okay, I still need to find out about Mom and Daniel and Andrew. I'm really worried about them, Dad!"

"Don't be, Megan. "Your mom isn't *in* Florida, and neither is your stepdad and stepbrother."

"How do you know that? If they're not there, then where are they?"

"Daniel and Andrew are with your Uncle Keith in Louisiana. So is your grandfather. But your mom's in Colorado. She came with me to look for you Megan, but I had to leave her in a safe place when I found out you were coming here. She's probably not too happy with me right now, but she's sure going to be thrilled to see you!"

Eric gave her a brief run-down of the details; how he'd first returned to Florida and looked for them at their home, and then what happened after he made his way to his father's place on the Caloosahatchee River. Megan was incredulous at all they had been through, and he barely gave her the half of it.

"You did all that for me? Mom took all those risks to come with you?" Tears were running down her cheeks as Eric pulled her close to him, wrapping his arms around her.

"Of course we did, Megan! You're our only daughter! There's nothing I wouldn't do for you. I'm just sorry I wasn't here to keep you from having to go through what you did in the first place."

"Now I'm worried about Mom *and* Aaron! Are you sure she's safe at that cabin? Anything could happen to them out there!"

"I don't know any place that's truly safe anymore, Megan, but I felt good about Bob's cabin or I wouldn't have left them there. I felt much better about that than I did about bringing them with me. It's in a remote area and not easy to find, and the three of them are well-armed. Your mom's a lot tougher than you may realize, Megan. And Jonathan will fight to the death for her. Vicky is a survivor too."

Megan showed little emotion when Eric told her what happened to Gareth. It was clear to him that whatever feelings she'd once had for him were long gone. Her concern now was for her family and her true friends, like Aaron. She wanted to be reunited with all of them now and wanted to know how they were going to make that happen. With her mom far to the north in that mountain wilderness, and Aaron's location unknown, Megan wanted to know what they were going to do next. But they were still in the room where Eric had been brought in to meet her, and Aaron's uncle and aunt that had been looking after his daughter since she arrived were still in there with them, waiting.

"You two are going to need a lot of time to catch up, and tell each other your stories," Ethan said to Megan. "Both of you are welcome at my house for as long as you'd like to stay. Let's go back there now and get away from this place. I'm sure your father has seen all he wants to see of it. You can discuss your plans there later and you know I will help you in any way I can."

Eric thanked him, and Megan agreed that would be a good idea. Eric walked her out of the room with his arm around her, and they were about to get into Ethan's pickup when Megan pointed at something out on the main road leading into town.

"Isn't that your other truck, Ethan?"

Ethan turned around and looked, squinting hard to try and see through the glare on the windshield as he watched the battered old Toyota heading their way. "That *is* my truck! Now, who would have the nerve to steal my truck and drive it straight to the police station with me standing right in front of it?"

Eric didn't know what to make of any of this until the truck skidded to a stop and the driver jumped out, causing him to reach for Megan's hand, in case it was some kind of attack. But Megan tore away from his grasp and went running straight towards the young man who'd been driving. He was tall and long-haired and clearly Apache, and he ran to meet Megan with open arms.

BOOKS IN THIS SERIES

ABOUT THE AUTHOR

Scott B. Williams has been writing about his travels and adventures for more than thirty years. His published work includes hundreds of print and online magazine articles and more than two dozen books. His interest in trekking, sea kayaking and sailing small boats to remote places led him to pursue the wilderness survival skills that he has written about extensively in both his fiction and nonfiction works.

A solo sea kayaking odyssey of nearly two years, undertaken at age 25, set Scott on his path to becoming a storyteller when he authored the account of that adventure in his 2005 travel narrative: *On Island Time: Kayaking the Caribbean.* That journey and countless others that took him far off the grid for extended periods gave him the inspiration to delve into his passion for fiction and to write action and adventure tales like the ones that shaped his own desire to travel and explore.

With the release of his first novel, *The Pulse,* in 2012, and the subsequent sequels to it that became a popular post-apocalyptic series, Scott moved into writing fiction full time. Later and ongoing projects include the *Dark-*

ness After series and the *Feral Nation* series, with more new works currently in development. To learn more about his upcoming books or to contact Scott, visit his website at: www.scottbwilliams.com

Made in the USA
Monee, IL
09 January 2023

24850623R00142